A MURDER OF CHRISTMAS PAST

THE KITTY WORTHINGTON MYSTERIES
BOOK FIVE

MAGDA ALEXANDER

HEARTS AFIRE PUBLISHING

CHAPTER 1

DECEMBER 1923

ON THE WAY TO A WEDDING

"*K*ITTY, YOU DON'T THINK WE FORGOT ANYTHING?" Mother asked for the fourth or fifth time. Since we'd boarded the Winchester-bound train at London's Victoria station, she'd been riddled with nerves. Unusual to say the least, for she was usually the calm in a storm. But then it wasn't every month her daughter was marrying a duke.

"No, Mother." She had a right to be concerned. The previous Duke of Wynchcombe, a penny-pincher of the worst sort, had spent precious little money on Wynchcombe Castle, so it was rather sparsely furnished. Since close to twenty-five guests were expected for the wedding, Sebastian, the current duke and my sister's fiancé, had given Mother and his sister, Lily, carte blanche to purchase whatever furnishings and decorations they deemed appropriate. As a result, we'd brought so many items along, a private luggage car had to be requisitioned for our sole use. And this was in addition to everything that had already been purchased and sent ahead.

"Margaret's wedding gown and trousseau?" Mother asked.

I plucked the list from my handbag. "Tucked away in two red trunks." Angelique, our modiste, had personally supervised the packing of the precious wardrobe.

"Linens and curtains for the beds? Towels and such for the bathrooms?"

Another glance at the list. "Four brown trunks packed and loaded." Since she wouldn't rest easy until she saw every item had been duly checked off, I handed the list to her.

She spent a few minutes perusing it before she breathed a sigh of relief. "I'm sorry to be a nuisance, Kitty, but I can't help but worry."

"Dearest" —I patted her hand— "understandably so. But everything has been well and safely stowed away. Margaret will have a truly splendid wedding."

Her shoulders eased as she settled back into her seat and gazed out the window. "I'm so glad we'll have our staff around us."

Given the magnitude of the wedding, Mother had deemed it necessary to have most of our London employees join us at Wynchcombe Castle in a few days' time.

"With them present, I know everything will be well and truly managed."

I had no doubt that would indeed be the case. We had an excellent staff, most of whom had been with us for years. They would leave no stone unturned to make sure everything would be just as it should be.

The door opened, and Owen Clapham, the former Scotland Yard detective inspector I'd hired to teach me investigative skills, stepped into our compartment. Not only had he been instrumental during two previous investigations, but he'd become a dear friend. Since Father and my brother Ned were busy with their investment firm, Worthington & Son, we'd asked him to escort us, for respectable ladies should not travel alone. Or so *A Lady's Guide to Etiquette and Deportment* declared.

"I've requested tea, ma'am," he said addressing Mother. "The waiter should come along any minute."

"Thank you, Mister Clapham. You are a treasure."

Settling in next to the window, he checked his pocket watch. "We're right on schedule. Barring any complications, the train should arrive on time."

"That's good to hear," I said.

Our arrival at Winchester proved to be a study in efficiency. We were met by our chauffeur, Neville, and Betsy, my former maid, who'd now become my assistant at the Ladies of Distinction Detective Agency, as well as Jack Seward, Sebastian's estate manager who'd been entrusted with transferring the items from the luggage car to the conveyances he'd brought from the castle. Since the process would take some time and the frigid weather was not conducive to standing around on a train platform, Mother and I opted to drive on ahead. Mister Clapham remained behind to provide whatever assistance he could.

"How are things at the castle, Betsy?" I asked as soon as we'd settled into the family's Rolls Royce which Neville had driven from London two days ago.

Betsy exchanged glances with Neville, her beau. "Well, Miss, since you ask, things are not quite as they should be."

Well, that was disappointing. "Such as?" I asked.

"To begin with, there is a problem in the kitchen."

"What kind of a problem?" Mother inquired, her brow knitting with concern.

"The kitchen, ma'am. His Grace had a brand-new AGA

gas stove delivered, but Mrs. Sweetwater, the castle cook, refuses to use it. She thinks it will blow up."

"But we hired Mrs. Branson to help her," Mother said. "Isn't she working out?" Mother and Lily had interviewed several candidates and sent the names of her top choices to Sebastian and Margaret. They'd hired Mrs. Branson, the best of the bunch, to assist the castle cook with the wedding preparations.

"Well, ma'am, when Mrs. Branson offered to show Mrs. Sweetwater how it works, she refused her help. So, the upshot of it is, all we've had to eat are cold meats, fresh fruits, and bread delivered from one of the town's bakeries."

"Well, we can't have that with a houseful of guests arriving in a week's time and a wedding feast to prepare," Mother said. "What did she use before?"

"An ancient iron stove. Unfortunately, a week ago it broke down beyond repair."

"Anything else?" Mother asked.

"I better not say, ma'am," Betsy said, a somewhat sheepish look to her face. "Miss Margaret will surely fill you in. Begging your pardon, ma'am."

Mother turned to me, a militant light in her eyes. "It sounds as if we've arrived not a moment too soon, Kitty."

"Indeed." If anybody could get the castle ready for a ducal wedding, it would be Mother.

The first sight of Wynchcombe Castle took my breath away. Magnificent in size, the concentric structure boasted no less than sixteen towers and numerous turrets and battlements, and, of course, a portcullis.

Mother seemed to be of similar mind. "Oh, my. It's rather grand, isn't it?"

"To put it mildly," I said.

"It would take a prodigious number of people to handle its upkeep."

"Which Lily said they don't have. Apparently, they have a difficult time retaining staff."

Betsy and Neville exchanged another glance. The words they did not utter spoke volumes.

There was a mystery there to be solved, that was for certain. As it turned out, there was more than one.

CHAPTER 2

WYNCHCOMBE CASTLE

*A*S WE DROVE THROUGH THE PORTCULLIS into the bailey, I couldn't help but be impressed. The castle's concentric architecture was comprised of outer walls, towers, turrets, and battlements, intended for defense, while the inner structure contained the great hall, kitchen, bedchambers, as well as additional rooms where the family entertained, and servants worked. As the Rolls came to stop in front of the inner building, its massive wooden door was thrown open by a burly footman.

A servant, who appeared to be eighty if a day, shuffled forward. His livery was one a butler would wear, but it seemed rather shabby and worn. Our own butler, Carlton, wouldn't be caught dead in such a rig.

Mother and I made our way inside the castle where Margaret and Lady Lily waited to welcome us, along with Lady Melissande, a recent friend of the family who'd become a dear friend to Lady Lily.

"Welcome to Wynchcombe Castle, Mrs. Worthington, Kitty," Lily said. Until the wedding was held and Margaret became the Duchess of Wynchcombe, she was the proper hostess.

"Thank you, dear."

"How was the train ride, Mother?" Margaret asked, after offering both of us a kiss on the cheek.

"Uneventful," Mother said glancing around the castle's interior. The great hall, at least sixty feet in length, with its high vaulted ceiling and tables lined along the right, left, and back of the room was an imposing sight, especially when one spotted the banners that hung from the ceiling bearing the ducal Wynchcombe standard. But, much as the butler, its appearance left something to be desired. The banners appeared dingy as if they hadn't been washed in an age, and the tables were thick with dust. But Mother, being Mother, took the high road. "It's rather impressive, isn't it?"

"It is," Lady Lily agreed. "Shall we step into the formal receiving room? I've ordered tea."

"Of course," Mother said.

"Please follow me," the octogenarian butler said.

We followed his slow, shuffling gait to a room where Georgian period furniture dotted the room. While the furniture itself sought to impress, much as the tables in the great hall, it was covered with dust.

Margaret waited only long enough for the butler to disappear before words tumbled out of her. "'Tis a disaster, Mother. I arrived two days ago from Oxford to discover the castle hasn't been cleaned in an age, and nothing you and Lily purchased has been set out."

Lily pinked up with embarrassment. "I apologize profusely, Mrs. Worthington. The housekeeper, Mrs. Rawlins, refuses to do any work. She claims she does not have sufficient staff."

"I got the same response from her," Margaret said with a huff.

"She got so used to doing as little as possible when Grandfather held the title," Lily said, "she resents having to do any work at all."

"Where are the furnishings we purchased?" Mother asked.

"She had them piled up in unused rooms in the castle's east wing."

"And soon there will be more, an entire luggage car's worth of furnishings which we brought with us. They'll need to be unloaded and placed somewhere."

"I'm so sorry," Lily said.

Poor thing was almost in tears.

"Dear Lily," Margaret rushed to say, "this is not your fault. You arrived barely two days ago yourself. How were you to know?"

"But it is my fault. I so wanted to make your and Sebastian's wedding a truly splendid event."

"And so it shall be, my dearest," Mother said.

She was interrupted from saying more by a maid who stepped into the room dressed in a uniform that was neither crisp nor clean. The tray she carried rattled with her every step. In all honesty, it appeared much too much for one person. So much so, she dropped it with a thunk on a round table in the center of the room.

"Thank you, Mary," Lily said, her face flushed.

"Ta, Miss," the maid said with a curtsy before fleeing the room.

She should have referred to Lily as Milady, not Miss.

"I apologize. The staff is not . . . trained," Lily said.

The tea was lukewarm at best, but the scones were surprisingly delicious. Once we'd drunk and eaten our fill Mother asked, "Where's Sebastian?"

"He's gone to London to attend to a financial matter," Margaret said.

"Probably arranging for your settlement," Mother said with a knowing smile.

"Settlement? As in money?" Margaret asked.

Mother nodded.

"But why? I don't need it. Father has already arranged a dowry for me."

"It's a gentleman's responsibility to provide for his wife and children. Once they come along, of course. And, heaven forbid, should something happen to him and you become a widow, he will want to see you lead a comfortable life with the funds he arranged for you. Sebastian would not be who he is if he didn't do this honorable thing."

"But, but—"

"It's best to allow men to have their way in this matter, dear. It makes them think they can command fate. They can't, of course, but it does make them feel better."

Margaret snorted. "Oh, Mother. You are a card."

"Now, Margaret, tell me about the kitchen problems."

"Mrs. Sweetwater has dug in her heels about preparing meals on the new gas cooker."

"Betsy told us she thinks it will explode," Mother said. "We certainly can't have unacceptable meals, so Mrs. Branson will need to take over the kitchen." She came to her feet and straightened her skirt as she readied for battle. "Now, let us go see how we can arrange things."

We arrived at the kitchen to find a strained atmosphere. A roly-poly of a woman with iron curls was hacking up fruit. The cook Mother had recommended, Mrs. Branson, was slicing bread, a bland look on her face. But her eyes as she glanced at us spoke volumes.

Once we got past the introductions, Mother flashed one

of her patented oil-over-troubled-waters smiles. "I under-stand you're leery of the new stove, Mrs. Sweetwater?"

"Yes, ma'am. It's the devil's contraption if you ask me." She cleaved through an apple so forcefully, a chunk flew clear across the wooden table.

Ignoring the mishap, Mother said, "I don't blame you for being leery of the new cooker. New things are quite scary at first. But I find once one gets used to them, things progress just fine."

Mrs. Sweetwater stopped the fruit massacre, wiped her hands on her apron, and finally gazed at Mother. There was pain in her eyes. "It's just I planned the menu for the festivi-ties on my old stove, ma'am. I don't know about the timing and such with the new one."

"Makes sense, ma'am," Mrs. Branson said. "An excellent cook, like Mrs. Sweetwater, would have doubts about using a new stove as she would want to provide excellent meals to His Grace and the wedding guests. Since I'm very familiar with the AGA cooker, I would be more than glad to *assist* with the meals and such. If Mrs. Sweetwater is amenable, that is." Apparently taking a page from Mother's book, she'd decided to pour sugar over the castle cook.

"Well, then, there you go." Turning back to the castle cook, whose ruffled feathers had been unruffled, Mother asked, "May I make a suggestion, Mrs. Sweetwater?"

"Of course, ma'am."

"Why don't you have Mrs. Branson demonstrate how to make a simple dish. Eggs, shall we say? How does His Grace like them?"

Mrs. Sweetwater straightened to her full height of five feet nothing. "The way any proper British duke does, ma'am. Poached."

"Of course. Mrs. Branson, why don't you show Mrs.

Sweetwater how to make a poached egg in the new cooker and you can go from there?"

"Be happy to, ma'am," Mrs. Branson nodded.

"Does that meet with your approval, Mrs. Sweetwater?" Mother asked.

"Yes, ma'am. Thank you, ma'am." Now that her dignity had been restored, a smile appeared.

"You are a wonder, Mother," Margaret said, once we'd exited the kitchen. "I don't know how you do it."

"I simply put myself in her place. She's not only afraid of the new cooker but that she will be replaced by someone younger than her. With Mrs. Branson's help, she'll soon lose her fears and learn how to manage the new stove."

"Now that that problem has been dealt with," Lily said, "would you like to go to your rooms, Mrs. Worthington, Kitty, so you can freshen up? We did manage to get your rooms cleaned."

"Of course, dear." As we climbed stairs that didn't appear to have seen a mop or a broom in quite some time, Mother asked, "And then we can go over your trousseau with your maid, Margaret. The trunks should be delivered soon."

"Ummm." Margaret hedged.

I knew that sound. It spelled trouble.

"Is something wrong?" Mother asked.

"My maid," Margaret said. "She's gone."

Mother came to a screeching halt on the landing. "Gone? Where?"

"Back to London."

Mother let out a deep sigh. "What happened?"

"She couldn't cope with the lack of decent meals, and a castle that has cold spots all over the place. And she claimed she saw the ghost of a woman crying out for her babe near the library."

Good heavens!

"Bound to be one or two specters in a castle this old." Mother said matter-of-factly. "Well, there's no time to find you a new one before the wedding. I'll ask Cummings to help. Between her and Grace, Kitty's maid, they can dress the three of us."

"Betsy can assist as well," I volunteered. My former maid, now receptionist at the Ladies of Distinction Detective Agency, would be thrilled to help us dress.

In the next hour, our luggage was delivered to our rooms, so we were able to bathe and dress. Supper turned out to be a lovely meal comprised of a simple roast, potatoes, and surprisingly tender asparagus in a white sauce. For dessert, fresh fruit was presented with an anglaise sauce. More than satisfied with the meal, we retired to the drawing room to enjoy coffee and tea. Lily did not remain long, as she was suffering from a headache. Lady Melissande bid us good-night as well.

"Given the state of the castle," Mother said, "we'll need the Worthington staff to join us earlier than I thought. We can't wait until the week before the wedding. There's too much to do. I'll telephone Carlton in the morning and arrange for him, Mrs. Simpson, and most of our staff to travel down the next day. We'll leave a skeleton crew behind so your father can get his meals and such."

"Yes, Mother." Margaret's usual vim and vigor seemed to have gone missing.

"Not to worry, dear," Mother said. "Everything will be fine."

"I don't see how. We barely have two weeks before the wedding, and the castle is a disaster."

"Comes from not having a duchess in place," Mother said. "But once you take on that role, you'll make sure everything is done properly. You'll have to hire a new housekeeper and butler, of course. But that's a matter for after the wedding.

The current ones can be retired with a nice pension at that time."

"The butler won't mind. He's always complaining about his aches and pains. Mrs. Rawlins is another matter altogether."

"She won't have a say, dear. You need a household that runs smoothly. We'll need more staff as well. Not London based, local ones, as they're more likely to stay. In the morning, we'll visit the nearest town and see if we can hire some."

"Yes, Mother." For the first time since we'd arrived, there was a light of hope in her eyes.

CHAPTER 3

HEADBOURNE WORTHY

*I*N THE MORNING, Neville drove us to Headbourne Worthy, the nearest village to the castle. I'd visited once before to talk to a witness from a previous investigation. Although she'd passed on to her glory, her niece, Mrs. Seaton, still lived there and agreed to talk to us.

After we explained our need, Mrs. Seaton suggested a number of people who would be eager to work at the castle, especially after Mother offered generous wages for anyone willing to stay until the New Year.

"Mind you," Mrs. Seaton said, "they wouldn't have set foot in Wynchcombe Castle when the old duke was still living. The man was a miserly sort who refused to pay half the time. But we've heard good things about the new duke from his farm hands."

That statement did not surprise me. Sebastian, a research fellow in agriculture at Oxford, held a deep love for the land.

So when he succeeded to the title, he made it his mission to ensure the farm, which grew a prodigious amount of grain, was well-managed. In that he was lucky, for his farm manager was a man who believed in applying modern agrarian principles. Together, they'd succeeded in growing a bumper crop of wheat, oats, and other grains this season. Apparently, Sebastian had become a favorite with the workers who saw him as a hands-on landlord, as opposed to his grandfather who was only interested in the money the crops would bring.

Before we said our goodbyes, Mrs. Seaton promised to spread the word that anyone who wanted a position should present themselves at the castle in the morning.

I, however, did not hold high hopes. It was the holiday season, after all. How many people would be willing to work through it? But I was pleasantly surprised the next day when a steady stream of individuals came through the castle gate. None was turned away as long as they convinced Mother and Margaret they were willing to put in the work. By late afternoon, we had a full assortment of maids, ranging from those who cleaned the chambers to kitchen and laundry ones. Nor were the men left out. Mother and Margaret hired not only footmen, but hall boys and a boot boy as well. As a result, the staff grew from half a dozen to over forty. Most wished to return to their homes at the end of their working days, but a dozen or so expressed a desire to reside in the castle, so rooms were assigned to them which given the state of those chambers were the first things they cleaned. All were promised full employment after the New Year if they worked to Margaret's satisfaction. Mother had made it very clear who their mistress would be.

Once the hiring process was completed, Mother charged one of the footmen with locating the housekeeper who was eventually found sleeping in her room. As always, Mother handled that conversation with her usual efficiency and kindness. "Mrs. Rawlins, you will need help for the wedding, so we've taken on the task of hiring additional staff from the local village. My housekeeper, Mrs. Simpson, will also be joining us tomorrow as you can't be expected to manage the additional staff by yourself."

Mrs. Rawlins pruned her lips, but her words were accommodating enough. "Very well, ma'am. Whatever you think best."

Once she left, I asked, "She was a little too willing to accept the new order of things, wasn't she?"

"'Tis an overwhelming task to prepare a castle for a ducal wedding," Mother said. "She's probably grateful her load has been lightened."

What load? I wanted to ask. The woman played least in sight most of the time. I didn't say a word, of course, as it would help matters not a whit.

The next day every one of our newly hired staff arrived bright and early. As we hadn't had time to order new livery, we'd arranged for black trousers and jackets with white shirts for the men, and white blouses and black skirts for the women. The local shopkeepers were extremely grateful for the business, since all apparel was being ordered from them. Once a final staff was chosen after the New Year, Wynchcombe Castle livery would be arranged for them.

Upon their arrival that afternoon, Mrs. Simpson and Mr. Carlton, our housekeeper and butler, immediately took command of the castle, ably aided by our London staff as well as the new recruits. The army of maids was sent to clean every room the guests would occupy as well as all the public rooms. Draperies were taken down as there would be no more use for them. The Great Hall banners, however, would need to be cleaned and rehanged, so the laundry maids were immediately put to work.

I wouldn't have believed it if I hadn't seen it myself, but three days later, a miracle had been wrought. Every guest bedroom had been swept and cleaned, its furnishings polished to mirror shines. Old mattresses and draperies had been burned, replaced with the new ones Mother and Lily had purchased. Carpets had been beaten within an inch of their lives. So many dust clouds had covered the maids, they'd needed to bathe after performing that onerous task. They'd been extremely grateful for the modern plumbing Sebastian had installed.

On the fourth day, Sebastian returned to a castle that now sparkled like the jewel it was meant to be. "I say, Mrs. W, you've done wonders." Of course he knew it was Mother's work for Margaret had kept him apprised.

"Oh, pshaw," she colored bright pink for she could never take a compliment. "Couldn't have done it without your newly hired staff, our butler, and the housekeepers." It was only our housekeeper that deserved the compliment for Mrs. Rawlins only showed up for meals and disappeared the rest of the days. After a couple of attempts to find her, we'd given up as no one had been able to locate her. Not that it mattered, as her position had been most assuredly forfeited. Mother had sent word to the London domestic employment agency we regularly used, and they'd already located highly qualified candidates to serve as housekeeper and butler for Wynchcombe Castle. After her wedding and before her return to Oxford for her Hilary term, Margaret would interview them.

The next day Father, Ned, and Robert, my fiancé, descended on the castle along with the first of the wedding guests. They'd made a party of it on the way down on the train for Lady Emma, and her mother, Lady Carlyle, as well as Lords Marlowe and Hollingsworth arrived as well. Of course, Father had brought Sir Winston as he was not about to leave his beloved hound behind.

"Welcome to Wynchcombe Castle," a beaming Sebastian exclaimed, his arm around Margaret's waist. "I trust the journey was uneventful."

"Absolutely," Father said.

"Well, except for the sheep that blocked the tracks," a disgruntled Lady Carlyle said. "It took a full half hour to clear them." As Lady Emma, my partner in the Ladies of Distinction Detective Agency, was on the guest list, we had to include her mother, Lady Carlyle. According to Mother, it would be a breach of etiquette if she hadn't been invited as well. Of course, Lady Carlyle readily agreed. She wasn't about to turn down an invitation to a ducal wedding, even if he was marrying a person with no blue in her blood. I just hoped she'd adopt a more amiable disposition as the days progressed.

As Carlton had arranged the order of things, the staff were soon collecting the guests' luggage to be transferred to their respective rooms. Sir Winston had been taken in hand by one of the footmen who would escort him to a warm spot in the kitchen where his bed had been laid out. While that was carried out, Sebastian invited the wedding party to step into the formal receiving room where he and Margaret could properly welcome them with wassail, food, and drink.

Robert and I remained for a short while, but we hadn't seen each other for the eternity of a week. So, after a few minutes of conversation with the newly arrived guests, we escaped to the Wynchcombe library to properly greet each other.

Threading his hand through mine, he gazed around the space. The library's size alone with its vaulted ceiling would awe anyone never mind the hundreds of books that resided on its shelves.

"Impressive, isn't it?" I asked, noting the wonder in his eyes

"To say the least."

Guiding him toward a deeper section of the library, I stroked some of the books on one shelf. Like most things in the castle, they hadn't been dusted for ages. "These are really old. Some date back to the sixteenth century. There are even manuscripts created by monks."

"Imagine that." His gaze returned to me as he took me into his arms. "I missed you."

"Not as much as I have," I said, returning his kiss. Caught up in the emotion, I leaned back against a shelf, and something clicked behind me. Turning toward the sound, I discovered an opening where a bare wall had been.

"What on earth?" I asked. "That wasn't there before."

Taking my hand, he led the way toward the opening and peered into it. "Looks like a priest hole."

I'd heard of them, of course. After Queen Mary's bloody reign, Queen Elizabeth turned the country back toward the Church of England and away from the Catholic faith. Subsequently, priests had been hunted down with many of them losing their lives. To save their clergy, Catholic families took to building priest holes in their castles and country houses to keep them from being captured and killed.

"I didn't realize that once upon a time the Dukes of Wynchcombe practiced the Catholic faith." They certainly did not now as Margaret and Sebastian's wedding would be presided over by Pastor Pennyworth, a Church of England minister and Mister Clapham's son-in-law.

"Given the punishments doled out to those who refused to give up Catholicism, many families chose to turn Protestant to keep their property and, indeed, their very lives." He pointed to the opening. "This appears to be a rather sizeable priest hole, though. They tended to be a tad smaller, barely large enough for a man to sit hunched over."

A thrill of excitement ran through me. "Shall we go exploring?" I was curious to see the space.

"We'll need some light." From the depths of his jacket, he retrieved a torch that resembled a flask more than anything else.

Laughter burst out of me. "Do you always carry one of those with you?"

"Pays to be ready." He held out his hand. "Shall I lead the way?"

He didn't have to ask twice, as I was always eager for his touch.

To my surprise, the opening led to a tunnel which was neither closed nor small. Indeed, the path was downright spacious—about three feet wide and a few inches over five feet high. Robert being slightly over six feet had to bend from the waist whereas I was almost able to stand up straight. The air smelt musty, as if fresh air hadn't been allowed to penetrate; and the path was indeed dark. So, I was glad for Robert's torch, even if the illumination did not provide much light. By necessity, we were forced to slow down as we didn't want to stumble and fall. For several minutes we continued our journey. Twice we encountered a wall; but an opening, once to the right, another to the left, showed us the way. Finally, after ten minutes or so, we were met by an arched door, beautifully carved with Christian symbols and secured by a metal handle that curved unto itself.

To my great relief, the handle turned easily, and we were able to pull the door open.

Once Robert flashed his torch around the space, we realized we were inside a chamber, similar in size to the smaller castle bedrooms. I blinked and coughed for the room contained a fair amount of dust. We carefully made our way around the chamber which didn't contain much. A wardrobe sat in one corner, its doors flung wide open. The few clothing pieces within it appeared feminine in nature. Strange, to say the least, if this space had been meant for priests. A modest table and two chairs, nothing like the Georgian furniture that graced many of the castle chambers, resided in the middle of the room. A padded kneeling stool, somewhat worse for the wear, rested in front of a crucifix high up on the wall. But the pride of place belonged to a four-poster bed. The drapes, which appeared to be fashioned from red velvet, had seen better days, but once upon a time they would have been beautiful.

"Well, priests who hid here would not have suffered. The furniture might not be of the best quality, but it's substantial," I said advancing toward the bed. "And they certainly had a gorgeous bed to sleep in. I grabbed one of the curtains and carefully pulled.

Robert's torch illuminated the bed and what rested on it. The remains of a female long ago dead.

CHAPTER 4

THE GAME'S AFOOT

"*D*EAR HEAVEN!" I said, crashing backward into Robert.

"Indeed."

Shaking with emotion, I dared a second look while the torch lit the figure from her head to her feet. The dress reached to her ankles. It would have been considered church wear once upon a time. "How long do you think she's been here?"

"A while." His voice rumbled in his chest. "We shouldn't touch anything else. Evidence will need to be collected."

"Yes, of course." His caution was unnecessary. Last thing I wanted was to handle anything else in that room while a dead body lay on the bed.

"We need to go back. The authorities need to be notified."

We made our way through the labyrinth until we emerged once more into the library. My gown and Robert's suit were covered with dust.

Still trembling, I pointed out the obvious. "We can't return to the drawing room looking like this. At the very least, we should brush ourselves off before we alert Sebastian."

"Best done in our rooms. Hopefully, we will not encounter anyone on the way."

But before we could act on our intention, Ladies Lily and Melissande entered the library. "There you are!" Lady Lily said. "Mrs. Worthington asked us to look for you as Lady Carlyle was making rather pointed remarks about your absence."

"I suggested you were probably giving Inspector Crawford a grand tour of the castle," Lady Melissande said with a smile.

We stepped out of the shadows fully into the light, for the first time enabling Lady Lily to clearly see us. "Good heavens. You look like you've fallen into a dustbin. What happened to you?"

As calmly as I could, I pointed toward the opening on the wall. "We found a priest hole, and we went exploring."

"Oh, how fun," Lady Melissande said. "Did you find anything interesting?"

"You might say that," Robert responded.

"Ooh, can we see?" Lady Lily took a step forward as if she intended to go through the opening.

"Better not, Lady Lily," Robert said.

"Whyever not?" Lady Melissande asked, a wrinkle to her brow.

I responded with the first thought that came to me. "It's not safe. We need to consult with Sebastian so he can determine what should be done. Can you ask him to step into the library? And please do it as discreetly as you can. We don't want to alarm the other guests. We can't do it ourselves. As dusty as we are, it's bound to cause comment."

Lady Lily hesitated but a moment before she said, "Of course. Come, Mellie."

It didn't take long for Sebastian to arrive. By his lonesome, thank heaven. "Lily said you wanted to talk to me." His gaze held a questioning look.

In as few words as possible, we explained what we'd found. Appalled, he followed Robert through the opening while I remained in the library to keep anyone from doing the same. It would not do to muck up whatever evidence existed.

I didn't wonder what he would do next. At the very least, he would contact the police. Realistically, we could not prevent word from leaking out about what we'd found, but it would be Sebastian's decision regarding how and when to share the news. Unfortunately, such a dreadful discovery was bound to affect the holiday festivities. I just hoped it wouldn't ruin his and Margaret's wedding day which was a little over a week away.

While I waited for Sebastian and Robert to reemerge, I dusted myself off as well as I could. By the time they returned, I was barely presentable, but at least I'd removed the cobwebs from my hair.

As could only be expected, Sebastian had a horrified expression on his face. "I can't believe that poor soul was lying in that room for ages, and not given a proper burial."

"It is sad indeed," I responded, sending up a swift prayer for the woman who'd laid on that bed for so long. "How do you wish to proceed?"

He combed a hand through his hair. "I'll need to notify the authorities, of course. Robert will accompany me to the study while I make that telephone call as he will know better than I how it should be done."

"Of course." I shot a graceful look toward Robert. "What do you wish me to do?"

Sebastian gazed at me with a pained expression. "I hate to leave this duty to you, but could you tell Margaret? Better clean yourself off before you do."

So much for me thinking I'd done a half-decent job. "Of course."

He turned to Robert. "Ready?"

Robert nodded.

After they left, I rushed up the stairs to my room. It wouldn't do to change, it would excite too much comment. So I had to satisfy myself with brushing my hair and dusting down my dress with a clothes brush. I did change my silk stockings as they'd been torn during our walk through the labyrinth. Once I deemed myself presentable, I rushed back the stairs to the drawing room.

Upon my arrival, Margaret gave me a pointed look while Mother provided one of her patented raised brows, but neither said a word. Lady Carlyle, on the other hand, couldn't hold her tongue. "Ah, there you are. We were wondering where you'd gone."

"Mother," Lady Emma hissed out.

Which did nothing to stop Lady Carlyle's vitriol from spilling out. "Did you lose Inspector Crawford?"

"He's making a telephone call. He'll be along soon."

"And His Grace?"

"Goodness, Lady Carlyle, aren't you the curious one?" Lady Melissande said in a tone that transmitted how very gauche.

"You appear a bit parched, dear sister," Margaret approached me with a container of some liquid in her hand. "Here, have some punch."

"Thank you." Gladly taking it, I drained half the cup.

"What's going on?" she whispered.

I nodded toward a corner of the room which was unoccupied at the moment. When we arrived there, I explained as well as I could what we'd found.

Other than a raised brow, she didn't react in any other way. "Sebastian?"

"He and Robert are calling the Winchester Constabulary. He'll explain things as soon as that is done."

"Yes, of course."

"What are you two whispering about?" Lady Carlyle asked from her perch on the sofa.

"The wedding, of course," Margaret answered.

We didn't have long for Sebastian and Robert to appear. After gaining everyone's attention, he explained what had been discovered, and that the authorities had been notified. They would be along momentarily.

"A dead body!" Lady Carlyle screeched. She turned to her daughter. "Emma, we must leave right away before we're murdered in our sleep."

"Now, Mother. I'm sure it won't come to that," Lady Emma said.

"I apologize, Lady Carlyle," Sebastian said, "I didn't make it clear. The remains are not . . . fresh. The deceased has been there for some time."

"How long?" she asked.

"The medical examiner will have to determine that," Robert said. "But it's fair to say that it's been there for a number of years."

"Heavens!" Mother said.

"Doesn't matter. I refuse to stay in a place where there's a dead body." Lady Carlyle clutched her daughter's arm. "Come, Emma, we're leaving."

I couldn't allow her to depart. If she did, she'd spread the news about the remains far and wide. In no time at all, the press was bound to get wind of it. They would descend on

Wynchcombe Castle and Margaret and Sebastian's wedding would be ruined. She had to be stopped.

I pasted on my brightest smile. "Now, Lady Carlyle, if you leave now, you'll never know *all* the facts. Wouldn't you rather stay and see the investigation to its conclusion?" As an inveterate gossip, she would want to learn every little tidbit so she could tittle-tattle about them to her heart's content. Not that I would allow that to happen. Somehow, I would find a way to draw her venom before she could strike.

Seemingly, everyone held their breath while she pondered my suggestion. But finally, she turned to me. "Well, you do have a point," she said in a much mellower tone. "We'll stay."

Lady Emma rolled her eyes. Not that she would have left with her mother. She would have simply put her on a train and said goodbye.

While we waited for the police to arrive, the gentlemen gathered in groups of two or three. The ladies, on the other hand, settled themselves in the sofas and settees that dotted the room pretending nothing had happened. Except for Mother, that is. She grabbed my arm and led me to the same corner where Margaret had stood. "Kitty, you must solve this right away. We can't make merry with this hanging over our heads. It's unChristian."

Margaret soon joined us. "What are you talking about?"

"Mother wants me to investigate the murder."

"I agree."

"Not you too!" I whispered a little too loudly and heads turned toward us.

"Speak softer, dear," Mother said.

"I know nothing about this person, whoever it is," I rushed to say. "I wouldn't know where to start."

"With the servants, of course. They know everything,"

Mother said. "Start with the housekeeper, the butler, and the cook. They've all been here a long time."

"But what if this person died even before they came on board?"

Mother pondered that question for a few seconds. And then she asked, "How were the remains clothed?"

"She was wearing a dress."

"So, it's a woman," Margaret said.

"Yes."

"What was the style of the dress?" Mother asked.

"Long. What was left of it reached her ankles."

"That doesn't help much. Was it fitted at the waist or loose?"

I forced myself to study the image imprinted on my mind. "Fitted."

"Not from the 1920s then. What about the sleeves?"

"Fitted as well."

"Not leg-of-mutton?"

"No."

"Late Victorian age then. No more than thirty years, I would say."

"Mother, you are a wonder," Margaret said.

"Yes, dear. That means, at the very least, Mister Cogsworth and Mrs. Sweetwater were in residence when she was here."

"You're assuming they knew her."

"Of course they knew her," Margaret said. "You just don't hide yourself in a priest hole without somebody arranging it. Unless there was another way out."

"Not that I could see, but of course it would have to be examined."

"Robert can do that," Mother suggested.

"He will not be able to do that," I hissed. He may have been a Chief Detective Inspector at Scotland Yard, but it didn't mean we could call upon him to exert himself. Searching for a reason to refuse Mother's suggestion, I offered the logical one. "He won't be put in charge of this investigation."

"Well, of course, dear." Mother patted my hand. "But he'll want his future sister-in-law to have a joyful wedding. He'll investigate."

"What are you discussing?" Lady Emma. She'd sneaked up on us.

"Mother wants me, and Robert, to investigate."

"And me. I'll need something to keep me busy so I don't commit matricide." To say the least, Lady Emma and her mother had a contentious relationship. After she'd failed to snag a husband during her season, Lady Emma had been informed by her family they could not afford a second one. Her sister Gloria would be brought out instead, leaving Lady Emma to rusticate in the country. Refusing to accept that horrid fate, Lady Emma had accepted my offer to partner with me in the creation and management of the Ladies of Distinction Detective Agency. When she informed her family she would not be returning to the country with them, a final rift had occurred.

"Lady Emma!" Mother exclaimed.

"Ahem." Lady Lily had also sidled up to us. "Whatever you're planning, count me in."

"Me too," Lady Melissande said.

Glancing to the side, I noticed Robert had been similarly accosted by Lords Marlowe and Hollingsworth, and my brother, Ned.

Sebastian and Father were doing their manly duty and keeping Lady Carlyle entertained.

I let out a heavy sigh. "Fine. We'll investigate. Tomorrow morning we meet in the library, well, maybe not the library." Seeing that was where the body was.

"The nursery, east wing, top floor, will be a better spot. Nobody will bother us there," Lady Lily said. "I'll tell Ned. He can talk to the other gentlemen."

"I'll leave it to all of you then," Mother said. "Margaret, Sebastian, and I will not participate in the investigation as we'll be busy with the wedding preparations."

Margaret looked as if she'd liked to object, but her common sense prevailed. "If you need anything at all, please let me know. And thank you, Kitty, and indeed all of you," Margaret said. "Sebastian and I are truly grateful."

CHAPTER 5

THE INVESTIGATIVE COMMITTEE MEETS

*A*FTER BREAKFAST THE FOLLOWING MORNING, we found our way to the nursery. Most of us, anyway. Some who remained nameless—Lord Marlowe and Lady Emma—took a couple of wrong turns and got lost. Or so, they said when they finally turned up. I, for one, was quite suspicious.

During our last investigation, it'd become quite evident they'd grown attached to each other. Instead of doing the sensible thing and becoming engaged, they'd decided to play games. Dangerous ones, if you asked me. But, as Lady Emma was so fond of reminding me, she knew what she was doing so I should kindly refrain from offering advice which was neither sought nor wanted. Heeding that admonishment, I did not comment when they finally joined us in the nursery, although I did offer a raised brow.

Since we needed to know the lay of the land before we

determined how to proceed, Robert provided us with a summary of the events from the day before.

After a cursory examination, the Hampshire medical examiner had determined that the woman did not die a natural death. Her skull had been fractured with a blunt instrument. In other words, she'd been murdered. He could not ascertain much more than that but arranged for the remains to be removed to his establishment so he could perform a postmortem.

Once the body was taken away, Detective Inspector Fallon from the Hampshire Constabulary performed a thorough search of the room. There wasn't much to investigate. A four-poster bed from which red tattered-velvet curtains hanged, a wardrobe which contained three dresses, one pair of shoes on a shelf, and undergarments in the lower drawers. A table with two chairs, built of good English oak, a crucifix affixed to the wall on the other side of the room in front of which a padded kneeling stool resided. And an empty cradle which rested against the bed.

"A cradle?" Lady Lily asked. "So she had a child with her?"

"So it seems. But, of course, we have no way of knowing. The cradle could have been stored there."

"Were there infant clothes in the wardrobe?" Lady Emma asked.

"No. The only thing that was there were the dresses, undergarments, and shoes."

"What was the quality of the materials? Could you tell?"

"I asked for, and received, permission to show them to Catherine so she could determine if they were quality or homespun."

Taking over the narrative, I said, "The dresses were made from plain cotton. In my opinion, they were the garments of a servant, both in their workmanship and style."

"And yet the bed curtains were made of velvet, an expensive cloth," Lady Melissande said.

"More than likely, the bed and the wardrobe predated the clothes," I said. "Maybe they were fashioned for an honored person, someone the family would value, such as a priest. Since Catholic priests were persecuted during Elizabeth Tudor's reign, the room was probably built to hide him."

"But we're not Catholic," Lady Lily said.

"Not now. But maybe you were once upon a time. Catholic families suffered terrible punishments for practicing their faith. Maybe a previous Duke of Wynchcombe felt it best to renounce his faith to keep his family and property intact. There would be records somewhere, I imagine. The library would be a good place to start."

"I was never allowed below stairs when I lived here," Lady Lily said. "My entire life was conducted on this floor. You see my grandfather did not wish to be reminded of my existence."

Lady Melissande pressed Lady Lily's hand. "I can help you look if you wish."

Lady Lily shook off her melancholy and smiled. "'Tis no matter. We'll be too busy with the investigation and wedding festivities to go in search of them. But they would probably be of interest to Margaret."

My sister, the scholar, would definitely be eager to know. "I'll mention it to her." Turning to Robert, I said, "Anything else?"

"I don't think Inspector Fallon is keen on investigating this murder. He said too much time has elapsed. Even if some of the staff here at the castle could shed some light on the matter, their memories could be faulty. Other witnesses could have left or passed away."

"Well, no matter what he thinks, we have to try."

"Hear, hear," Marlowe said.

"So how do you want us to proceed?" Lady Emma asked.

After a quick glance at my journal, I said, "I jotted down some likely avenues of investigation. First and foremost, the staff. The butler, the housekeeper. And Mrs. Sweetwater, the cook. They might know something. I'll talk to them."

"Very well," Lady Emma said.

"The residents of Headbourne Worthy might know something as well. We'll need to question the ones we hired, but we should focus on the older women and men. "Now, Lady Emma. There's bound to be a sewing circle or a women's institute in the village. I suggest you head over there and find out."

"Consider it taken care of," Lady Emma said.

"Lady Melissande, with your convent upbringing, you're bound to know your way around a church. Visit the parish church, talk to the priest. I have no idea if he's young or old. Maybe the church ladies, the church secretary if they have one, the church board. You get my drift."

"I do."

"Lady Lily, you're bound to have many responsibilities for the wedding, which means you'll be working with the current staff we just hired. Strike up conversations with them. They're too young to have personally witnessed anything, but maybe a parent, aunt, or grandmother mentioned something about the disappearance of a servant at the castle."

"I'll be glad to take on that task," Lady Lily said with her usual sunny disposition.

"Now, Lords Marlowe and Hollingsworth, the local pub will be your hunting ground. Alcohol loosens the tongue wonderfully, so spread your largesse and pay for a few rounds."

Both gentlemen nodded.

"Robert. You will visit Inspector Fallon and ask him to

keep you apprised. Praise his investigation even if he's not doing anything. Offer to help. There might be records of a missing person from long ago. I would say from twenty to thirty years past or so."

"Be glad to," he said with a twinkle to his eye. I got the feeling he enjoyed seeing me in charge.

"Ned. I'd like you to examine the castle records, the financial ones in the same time frame I just suggested to Robert. Sebastian's estate manager should be able to provide access to them. What's his name, Lady Lily?"

"Jack Seward."

"That's right. We met him at the train station. But with all the excitement, I forgot. Assure Mister Seward that Sebastian has given you permission, and you're not questioning his actions."

"Will do."

"What do you want me to do?" Mister Clapham asked.

"For now, see what information you can pick up at the local shops, including the post office. We only have eight days before the wedding so we'll need to start today. We'll meet again tomorrow afternoon. That should give you a day to pick up whatever information you can. Any questions?"

Nobody said a thing.

"Fine. Off you go."

"So, who are you going to talk to first?" Lady Emma asked.

"The housekeeper."

"Good luck finding her," Lady Lily said.

"Oh, I've devised a plan to find her hiding place."

After a sumptuous luncheon, the committee members started their investigations. While Ladies Melissande, Lily, and Emma were driven into Headbourne Worthy by our chauffeur, Lords Hollingsworth and Marlowe borrowed one of Sebastian's automobiles to travel to the village, taking

Mister Clapham along for the ride. If they both had too much to drink, as was likely, he could drive them back. Since today some of the staff had been asked to clean the chapel, Lady Lily decided to start there with her questioning. Ned would approach Mister Seward to go over the castle books.

I would start with Mrs. Rawlins, the castle's housekeeper. The night before, I'd asked one of the new maids responsible for dusting and such to keep tabs on her. If noticed, she would have an excellent reason for being in any part of the castle. She hadn't failed me.

I found Mrs. Rawlins where I thought I would—the solar, a sunny room located in one of the castle turrets. Luxurious and comfortable did not begin to describe it. Meant for small intimate family gatherings, it boasted of its own fireplace, a table and chairs where loved ones could eat, tapestries on the walls, rugs on the floor, and bookshelves replete with books. In other words, a cozy hideaway. She was reclining on a sofa, a blanket over her feet, reading a book.

"Mrs. Rawlins, how pleasant to see you. Enjoying the sun?"

Eyes widened as she sat up in a rush. "How did you find me?"

"Oh, I have my ways." I took a seat on a stuffed leather chair close to her. "Have you heard about the remains we discovered yesterday?"

She didn't try to claim ignorance. "Of course. The staff couldn't stop talking about it at dinner."

Word had indeed gotten out. But then there was no hope it wouldn't.

"Excellent. His Grace has asked me to find out as much as I can about the identity of the victim. All I know right now is she was a female. Do you have any idea who it could be?"

"Well, if I had to put a name to her, it would be Daisy Gordon."

I opened my journal and noted the name. "Why would you think that?"

"I wasn't employed here at the time, mind you. But I heard the stories from other servants when I came to work at the castle."

"And what did you hear?"

"She worked here as a maid, a flighty thing from what I heard, more cotton than brains inside her head. I was told she was pretty, easily caught men's eyes. Liked to flirt with them as well. Well, she must have done something she shouldn't because next thing they knew, there she was with a full belly."

"That must have been devastating for her."

"It was her own fault if you ask me. I always tell my maids, no shenanigans. Keep yourselves to yourselves. If you find yourself in the family way, you'll be dismissed."

"All two of your maids." After Mother and I arrived, we discovered there were only two of them to clean the entire castle. Not nearly enough.

"Well, I can't be blamed if that's all who was willing to work here. The old duke was a penny-pincher of the worst sort."

"But the new duke is not." After Sebastian inherited the title, there would have been plenty of time for her to ask him to increase the staff salaries. She hadn't done so. Probably because more servants meant more work for her. And that she was clearly not willing to do. "But that is neither here nor there. What happened to Daisy?"

"The old duke returned to the castle in the fall. When he found out she was expecting, he dismissed her. And that's all I heard. As I said, I wasn't working here at the time."

"When was this?"

"About twenty-five years ago. Daisy had been gone about five years or so."

"Very well." I shut my journal since I would get no more out of her.

"What's going to happen to my position?"

"That will be up to His Grace and my sister to decide."

"I'm too old to find another position. No one will want to hire me."

Maybe she should have thought about that sooner. "Sebastian and Margaret will not put you out in the cold. If they do decide to terminate your employment, they'll make arrangements."

"A nice pension?"

"Maybe." I was pretty certain they would, but I couldn't speak for them. "In the meantime, you might want to apply yourself. There's plenty that needs to be done."

Reclining back on the sofa, she picked up her book again. "I'll think about it."

That's all she was bound to do. Think. It was not likely she would stir herself.

CHAPTER 6

KITTY QUESTIONS THE STAFF

*T*HE NEXT PERSON ON MY LIST was the butler, Mister Cogsworth. I found him in the butler's pantry, fast asleep, a half empty whisky bottle on the shelf next to him. I rattled the doorknob, stomped my feet to no avail. He would not wake. Finally, I was reduced to jostling his shoulder. "Mister Cogsworth."

He came awake in a rush, his face in full panic. "What?" He look around confused. "Is the castle on fire?"

"No. I'm sorry to wake you, but I have some questions."

He cleared his throat, tried to struggle to his feet.

"No need to stand, Mister Cogsworth." I found a rickety looking chair, tested it to ensure it would hold my weight. Only when I felt it would did I accommodate myself.

All wrinkled brow, Mister Cogsworth blinked at me. I had no more than two minutes to ask questions before he nodded off again.

"Mister Cogsworth, Thank you for talking to me."

"My pleasure, Miss . . ." He blinked again.

"Worthington. I'm the future Duchess of Wynchcombe's sister."

"Oh, yes." He nodded.

I didn't know how much information I could obtain from him, but I had to try. "You've heard about the remains that were found?"

"In the priest hole. Yes."

That was a positive sign. "It was a female, poor soul. We're trying to determine who it was."

"Daisy Gordon. The old duke dismissed her because she was in the family way. A sweet thing she was. Always had a smile on her face. A hard worker too."

Glad to have Mrs. Rawlins' account confirmed, I pressed on, "Were you working here at the time?"

"Oh, yes. Must have been 1892, 93."

"So about thirty one years ago."

"Something like that."

"What happened to her?"

"She got in the family way, and the old duke dismissed her. I was sad to see her go."

"Did you in fact see her go?"

"Oh, yes. I had to escort her out of the castle. Broke my heart it did. She was such a sweet thing. It being late November and all. Close to Christmas it was. It was very cold that day. Remember like it was yesterday."

"You saw her walk away."

"Yes, Miss. She only had a small bag to hold her things. It broke my heart. She was such a sweet thing."

He was repeating himself.

"Do you know who the father was?"

"One of the footmen, John Stirling. Not that she ever said. She was such a sweet thing."

Obviously, I wouldn't get more out of him. "Thank you, Mister Cogsworth."

"You're welcome, Miss . . . "

"Worthington."

"You're marrying His Grace!"

"No, my sister Margaret is. I'll leave you to it then."

"Yes." His head bobbed forward and just like that he was fast asleep.

My last interview was with the castle cook, Mrs. Sweetwater. As she was in her early sixties, she was closer in age to Mrs. Rawlins, but younger than Mister Cogsworth. Unlike him, she had all her faculties. I arrived in the kitchen to find her going over the evening's menu with Mrs. Branson. Acknowledging how busy she was, I begged her for a few minutes of her time and she readily consented. After arranging for some tea and biscuits to be brought to us, she led me to her private parlor.

The place was as cozy as could be with a desk, two comfy chairs, and a cot. The staff quarters were located three flights up on the other side of the castle. Fine for evening slumber, but too far to travel when you needed a short rest.

"This is where I usually plan my menus for the week," Mrs. Sweetwater said. "By myself. I'm glad a new duchess will be here. I'm looking forward to discussing meals with her."

"I'm sure Margaret is looking forward to it as well." Margaret would rather have every tooth in her head pulled than discuss menus. She was not a domestic sort. But Mother had trained her well and she would do her duty, if for no other reason than to keep the castle running smoothly.

"How are the wedding banquet preparations coming along?" Might as well turn her up sweet.

"Splendidly. I must say Mrs. Branson has been a great

help. We should be able to present His Graces with a splendid wedding feast and a grand Christmas Day spread."

Sebastian was planning a Christmas Day celebration in the Great Hall. Not only were the wedding guests invited but so was every resident of Headbourne Worthy.

"How wonderful," I said. "Forgive me for bringing up a sad topic. You are aware about the remains that were found yesterday?"

"Yes, 'tis all the staff can talk about."

"Do you have any idea who it is?" I already had confirmation from Mister Cogsworth but another one wouldn't hurt.

"Daisy Gordon. The lass worked here as a maid about twenty nine or so years ago. A hard worker, but she also liked to flirt with the lads. Many were that attracted to her."

"Including John Stirling?"

Her brow furrowed. "Now how did you learn about him?"

"Mister Cogsworth."

"He would know, of course, as John was one of the footmen. He was smitten with her. Made a fool of himself whenever she was around."

"I understand she was expecting."

"Yes, she got herself in trouble, poor lass."

"And John Stirling was the father?"

"Oh, heavens no. She thought he was rather sweet, but she had no interest in him. Somebody else caught her eye. Someone who did not reside in the castle."

"Do you know who it was?"

"No. She didn't say. Even after the old duke dismissed her, she never revealed his name."

"Mister Cogsworth said he escorted her from the castle one day in late November."

"It was barbaric what the old duke did to that girl. Whatever sins she'd committed she did not deserve to be put out that frigid night and her with a full belly."

No, she didn't. Nobody deserved that. "Was that the last you saw of her?"

"No, dearie. It wasn't."

It was my turn to frown. "What do you mean?"

"She found her way into my kitchen through the back door. The one that leads to the castle gardens where we grow produce. She begged me for food before she went on her way. Well, it had started to snow and was beyond frigid. I simply could not let her go out in that. She would freeze before she found shelter. So, I hid her in the priest hole."

That surprised me. "You knew about it?"

"Mister Cogsworth, Mrs. Grimes, the old housekeeper, and I did. No one else was aware that it existed."

"How did you find out?"

"That knowledge had been passed down through the years from chatelaines to housekeepers, from cooks to cooks. They made sure the next person to take on those responsibilities knew."

"And yet, Mrs. Rawlins did not."

"She was hired after Mrs. Grimes was dismissed. So there was no opportunity for Mrs. Grimes to share the information with her. Just as well. Neither Mister Cogsworth nor I deemed her worthy of having that knowledge. More than likely, she would have sold that secret to one of the London newspapers. They're always harping about the aristocracy."

I had to agree with her about the gossip rags as I had good cause to know. And Mrs. Rawlins was not only lazy but seemed greedy.

"How did Daisy survive in the priest hole?"

"Mrs. Grimes, John Stirling, and I took care of her needs. Mrs. Grimes made her as comfortable as she could. I prepared generous food portions and had John Stirling deliver her meals."

"Mister Cogsworth didn't know?"

"He was three sheets to the wind most of the time. It was easy to hide her from him. We figured we would keep her hidden until the babe was born, and then we would find her a place to stay. The babe was not due until January, but it came in early December. A small tiny thing. A boy. She named him John since John Stirling had been of so much help to her. She loved her child, took very good care he didn't cry. But then that Christmas Eve, the babe's cries were heard, and the duke found out we'd hidden her. Before I could take the blame, Mrs. Grimes confessed. He dismissed her on the spot. When we went looking, we found the poor mite screaming for all he was worth, red faced, soaked in his nappies. Daisy was dead."

"Dear heaven! What happened to her?"

"That devil forbade us from touching her and ordered John Stirling to get rid of the babe. He was expecting guests you see, and he didn't want them to hear the babe's cries. They would think it was his. His duchess, bless her soul, had passed away by that time. So John took the babe. I packed as much food as I could, gave him all the money I had, and told him to take the babe to a woman in the village who'd lost her own child. She could feed the mite until he could drink milk on his own. And then John was gone."

"What about Daisy? Why wasn't she given a proper burial?"

"The old duke didn't want the scandal. So he closed the door and made me swear I would never enter it again."

"And you agreed?"

"What choice did I have? He would have dismissed me as well. Mrs. Grimes had a sister who would take her in, but I had nowhere to go. It was wicked of me, I know. I expect I'll pay for it some day."

"Mister Cogsworth never found out?"

"No. Mrs. Grimes had already left. And I never told him. John Stirling, of course, was already gone."

"Did you hear from him again?"

"No. But the wet nurse I suggested left town, almost overnight. In the company of a stranger, I was told."

"You think she and John Stirling left together?"

"Maybe. I had no way of asking without raising suspicion. She never returned. That much I know."

"Where did John Stirling hail from?"

"I have no idea. He never talked much about his home. He and his father had had a falling out."

No help there. But maybe Ned would have better luck with the books from the estate. "Has Inspector Fallon questioned you?"

"No."

"If he does, be careful what you say. I wouldn't want you to get into trouble."

"You're a kind soul, Miss Worthington, like your Mother and sister. But if he asks, I will tell him the truth."

Frankly, I feared for Mrs. Sweetwater's safety. She was the one who remembered the most. The murderer, whoever he or she was, could very well think her a threat and deal with her the same way he'd dealt with Daisy—by murdering her.

CHAPTER 7

A NIGHT OF CHRISTMAS SPIRIT AND SONG

FINISHED WITH MY INTERVIEWS, I found my way to the personal parlor Margaret had made available to me. There I would organize my notes while I waited for Hollingsworth, Marlowe, and Mister Clapham to return. I'd asked the footman standing guard at the castle entrance to show them to the parlor when they arrived, as I wanted to let them know about tomorrow's meeting. It'd gone past seven before they returned.

To my surprise, Hollingsworth and Marlowe weren't drunk as the proverbial lords. Although Marlowe did seem slightly tipsy and smelled of strong spirits. Mister Clapham, on the other hand, appeared sober as a judge.

"How did you fare at the pub?"

"Wunnerful," Marlowe slurred, slinging an arm around Hollingsworth's shoulders and swaying on his feet.

Maybe he was a bit tipsier than I believed. "You'll have to tell us about it tomorrow morning. Our meeting is at ten."

"Ten!" Marlowe objected. "The birds aren't up that early."

"Well, you'll have to be. Now, cocktails will be served in half an hour. You might want to, er, wash up." He couldn't come to the supper table reeking of alcohol. "Afterwards, we'll be attending a Christmas concert at the village." We might be in the middle of a murder investigation, but the Christmas traditions would still be observed. "We will be traveling in sleighs so wear something warm."

"Yes, ma'am." Marlowe saluted me.

"Don't worry, Kitty," Hollingsworth said. "I'll ring for his man. He'll be shipshape and Bristol fashion by the time dinner is announced."

"If you don't mind, Miss Worthington," Mister Clapham said. "I'll join the staff for supper."

"You're a guest, Mister Clapham," I reminded him.

"I appreciate you seeing me that way. But I might be able to learn something they're not willing to share with you or Lady Lily."

"Umm, you do have a point. Very well. We'll see you tomorrow at ten."

"Until then." And with that, he was off.

We sat fourteen for supper that night in the castle's formal dining room. We'd been joined by William Darrow, and his sister, Eliza, close friends of Sebastian from Oxford. The meal was a merry affair as the food was excellent and the wine freely flowed. Seated between Robert and Marlowe, I kept a close eye on the latter to make sure he didn't drink too much. But I need not have worried. He seemed to be moderating himself.

After supper, we gathered our winter coats, scarves, and gloves, and made our way out the castle gate where four horse-drawn sleighs awaited to take us to Headbourne Worthy for the Christmas concert. After arranging ourselves on the conveyances, the horses were given their heads. Soon the jingle jangle of bells on their harnesses were ringing merrily through the night. Although it was cold, I didn't feel it as I was tucked tightly against Robert who kept me quite warm.

The ride did not take long, and soon we were being welcomed into the Church of St. Swithun, which dated from the 11th century. Before the concert started, we were given a quick tour of the church, something that Margaret had prearranged. As we were shown into the vestry, she pointed out a stone carving.

"It originally stood on the outside of the original west wall."

"It appears . . . damaged?" I said.

"Unfortunately, it was vandalized during the Reformation, but you can still see the crucified Christ, St. Mary, and St. John."

Murmurs of appreciation rang through our group.

Once we were ensconced in our seats, I was more than happy to sit and observe. The air was redolent with incense as if the walls themselves had absorbed the heady scent. The altar had been gaily decorated with poinsettias, holly, vine, and Christmas candles. The children, about twenty in all, stood to the side of the altar. They seemed to range in age from seven to twelve and were dressed in red jumpers over white shirts, collar points peeking out from beneath. As I watched, a gap-toothed child smiled and madly waved at someone in the crowd.

I pointed him out to Robert. "He's adorable, isn't he?"

He smiled down at me. "They all are."

Tears sprang into my eyes as I imagined our own child, in a church such as this, waving madly at us.

Robert, being Robert, immediately sensed my change in mood. "Anything wrong?"

I threaded my hand through his. "On the contrary. Everything's right."

Raising my hand to his lips, he kissed it, causing my breath to hitch.

We didn't have time for more as the choral director, and the choir, were introduced. And then the heavenly sound of *Silent Night* filled the space. From there they proceeded to *Good King Wenceslas*, *While Shepherds Watched*, *We Three Kings of Orient Are*, *Deck the Halls*, and other songs, finishing with *We Wish you a Merry Christmas* with everyone invited to sing along. At the end, the entire congregation stood and cheered while the children rightfully took triumphant bows.

Full of Christmas joy and spirit, we climbed back into our sleighs. The return trip somehow was accomplished much faster. So, in no time at all, we were back at the castle.

After handing off our outer garments to the staff, the ladies headed into the drawing room to enjoy hot tea and chocolate along with assorted holiday treats and warm themselves by the cozy fire. The gentlemen wandered toward the billiard room to play pool, smoke cigars, and no doubt, partake of some whiskey. Since it'd been a full day, and tomorrow promised more of the same, none of the ladies remained long. We were soon bidding goodnights and meandering off to our rooms.

I arrived at mine to find Grace, who'd taken over maid duties from Betsy, happily reading on one of the chairs.

"Grace, thank you for waiting for me."

"It's my pleasure, Miss." Her eyes were big and bright. "I borrowed one of the books from the library. I hope that's allowed."

"Of course. Books are meant to be read." I turned my back to her, so she could unbutton my dress.

"I was curious about that priest hole," she said, "so I looked for something that talked about them."

After slipping out of my gown, I turned back to her. "Did you find one?"

"Yes, Miss. A board-bound one, covered with leather and fastened with metal clasps. That's what got my attention. It was so very unusual. I pried open the clasps, so very carefully. And, oh, Miss, it was a journal of sorts, written by the gentleman who built the priest hole."

I gasped. The priest hole had to have been built in the late sixteenth century. A book that old could fall apart merely by handling it. I pointed to the one she'd been reading. "It's not that one?"

She hitched up her chin. "No, Miss. That's one of me own. Bought with me own money."

My careless remark had hurt her feelings, the last thing I wanted to do. "I apologize. I spoke without thinking. I should have realized it wasn't the same book. Where's the one you found?"

"I thought it best if I took it to my room. To keep it safe. It's very fragile, but I was ever so gentle with it."

I squeezed her hands as a sign of approval. "I'm sure you were. I'll need to see it."

"Yes, Miss. I thought you would." She lowered her voice as if she were sharing a secret. "The thing of it is, it has drawings. And oh, Miss, he built another way out."

CHAPTER 8

INTO THE WOODS

*N*EEDLESS TO SAY, the next morning everyone was agog with excitement about the book Grace had found. We'd determined Margaret would oversee the handling of it. Not only would it be part of her future history, but she was the one true scholar in our midst. While Sebastian was knowledgeable about plants and such, he knew nothing about rare manuscripts. But Margaret had taken a seminar in rare books at Oxford. Although no expert, she was the one best suited for the task.

"As rare as this book is, it should be donated to Oxford," Margaret said. "They would know how best to preserve it."

"I agree," Sebastian said.

"At the moment, however," I said, "we need it to reveal its secrets. Grace said an illustration showed another way out of the priest chamber."

The book rested on a cloth that had been spread over a nursery table. Margaret carefully unclasped it and opened it to the front page. The flyleaf read "Priest Chamber at Wynchcombe Castle, Notations and Illustrations." No author was mentioned, but the date was—1593.

"It's a wonder someone created such a journal," Sebastian said, "given hunters were searching for and executing priests at the time."

"I imagine it was well hidden," Margaret responded. "Once the danger passed, someone added it to the shelves."

"Does a book catalog exist?" Lady Emma asked.

"No," Margaret said. "But Sebastian and I both agree one must be created. We will be hiring a librarian to do just that."

Wynchcombe Castle had been largely ignored by the old duke, who'd spent the bulk of his time in London. Sebastian and Margaret, however, planned to split their time between London and Hampshire. They would restore the castle to its former glory and leave a lasting legacy for future generations.

She'd brought a pair of tweezers. It was the gentlest of ways to handle the fragile vellum in the board-backed book. As Margaret turned the pages, we could see the ink was barely visible, only the occasional word could be read. We had better luck when we came to the illustrations.

The labyrinth we'd followed was precisely laid out with measurements between each section until it reached the chamber itself. Oblong in shape, it measured eighteen by twenty-four feet. Whoever hid there would not have suffered for lack of space. The room lacked windows, but holes had been drilled into walls. Robert had guessed they were for the conduction of air, so whoever resided there would not suffocate.

"There's no fireplace," Margaret said. "It must have been dreadfully cold."

"It was meant to be only a temporary measure," Sebastian

said. "I imagine they provided blankets and such to keep the priests warm."

"But Daisy lived there for a month or more," Margaret said. "She must have suffered dreadfully, and her babe as well."

Sebastian laid a gentle hand on Margaret's arm. "She's beyond suffering, dearest. All we can do is get her the justice she deserves."

Margaret squared her shoulders. "Yes, you're right." She pointed to a corner noted in the illustration. "I think this is the other exit."

"That's where the wardrobe stands," I said. "No wonder we didn't see it."

Margaret turned over more pages, but the book did not reveal any more secrets, at least none we could discern. "I think that's all we'll find," she said, standing up.

"It's enough, more than enough," I said. "We'll need to see where the second exit leads."

Sebastian placed his arm around Margaret. "This afternoon we'll be retrieving the Yule log and gathering ivy and holly to decorate the castle. We would love to make a party of it, but we understand if some can't make it due to the investigation. For those who wish to join us, we will be gathering at two in the Great Hall."

"How wonderful," I said. Something festive to anticipate.

After Sebastian and Margaret made their way out, I provided a summary about my interviews with the three members of the staff, we moved on to what Ned had discovered. I'd alerted him as to the footman's and housekeeper's names and asked him to find their records in the estate books. As always, he'd been successful.

"John Stirling hailed from a village not too far from here—Kings Worthy. I've asked Mister Clapham to gather what information he can."

"I've sent a telegram to the local constable," Mister Clapham said. "Once I hear from him, I'll know how to proceed."

"Thank you." I turned back to Ned. "Did you discover any information about Mrs. Grimes?"

"She left her employment on December 24, 1893, as did John Stirling. She hailed from London. Apparently, she managed the city's Wynchcombe household as well as the castle's."

Why pay for two housekeepers when one would do? The old duke had a lot to answer for, but then that was the least of his sins. His atrocious action toward Daisy's remains, never mind the way he'd treated Sebastian and Lady Lily, topped the list.

"Was there a mention of her next of kin?"

"None that I could find."

"Then let's hope Mister Clapham is successful."

"I'll do my best, Miss Worthington," Mister Clapham said.

"What about your journey into Headbourne Worthy? Did you discover anything?"

"Nothing until I came across the postmistress. She's served in that position for thirty-five years. She remembers Daisy. A very pretty young woman who drew the eye of many a man. She flirted with them all, whether they were married or not. Got her into trouble with some of the wives."

"I heard that as well from the sewing circle ladies," Lady Emma added. "No better than she should be was the general consensus."

"The church flower lady was a bit kinder in the way she phrased it," Lady Melissande said, "but the sentiment was the same."

"Any man in particular?" I asked.

"The vicar's son. He was a wild one, apparently. But he

54

couldn't have been the father. He left a year before Daisy disappeared."

"Lords Hollingsworth and Marlowe, did you discover anything?"

"The younger gents had plenty to say," Marlowe volunteered. "Apparently, they'd heard chapter and verse about Daisy from their mothers. Didn't hear a peep from the older ones, though."

"Probably because they were the ones involved."

"One of the sewing circle ladies approached me after I made my way back to the street," Lady Emma said. "She's too young to have known Daisy, but an aunt of hers had held a great deal of rancor toward her. Apparently, her aunt blamed Daisy for the loss of her beau. Not only that, but after Daisy was through with him, she tossed him away."

"Who was the beau?"

"The village constable. The aunt was quite bitter about it as she never married."

"What was the officer's name?"

"Constable Clemson. He died shortly after Daisy's disappearance."

"No help there then. What about her aunt?"

"She perished from the Spanish flu."

"How sad." So many people had died from that awful disease, including my sister Emily. That loss had almost destroyed Mother.

Chasing away the dark thoughts, I turned to Robert. "What did you discover?

"As I thought, Inspector Fallon is in no hurry to investigate. And the coroner is in no rush to hold an inquest, either. They postponed everything until after the New Year."

"Did they give a reason?"

"*The remains have laid on that bed for thirty years. A few more weeks won't hurt.'* That's a direct quote from Inspector Fallon."

"I don't understand that attitude given Sebastian is the Duke of Wynchcombe. You would think they would want to get in his good graces."

"They did make a logical argument. As it's the holidays, they would not be able to move things along as quickly as they wished. Not that I agree with it. After the first of year, I'll follow up with the Winchester Constabulary to ensure they do their duty."

"Thank you, Robert." I glanced at my journal to recall what else I'd asked him to do. "Were you able to examine the books?"

"I was. There were no reports of anyone gone missing at the castle."

"Unfortunately, that makes sense. The duke would have simply said all three employees resigned." I sighed. "Well, I believe that's everyone. Does anyone have anything else to report?"

Nobody did.

"Thank you everyone for your efforts. Sebastian and Margaret truly appreciate everything you've done. Luncheon should be served shortly. Afterward, I suggest we meet in the Great Hall and join the festivities. We'll meet here tomorrow at ten to hear Mister Clapham's report."

That afternoon we headed toward the woodlands to collect the Yule log which would burn in the Great Hall's fireplace and the holly and ivy to be hung there as well.

It would take fifteen minutes or so to reach the woods where the Yule log was to be collected. As his outdoor staff would do most of the work under the supervision of his estate manager, all that we would be required to do was eat, drink, and be merry. After our hard work with the investigation, we were all more than ready to do just that.

It was with much excitement we descended from the sleighs. The tree they'd chosen was indeed massive, but it had already been felled. All that needed to be done was carve out the lower part and load it into a contrivance they'd brought along. They would return the next day to retrieve the tree which would be erected in the Great Hall to be decorated by us.

Chairs were, of course, not available but there were logs and stumps aplenty on which we could sit. Servants cheerfully brought round trays laden with all manners of food and glasses filled with mulled wine. Robert and I found a stump not too far from where the Yule log was being retrieved where we could enjoy a bit of privacy.

I shivered for the temperature was dropping.

"You're not cold, are you? I can fetch a rug from the sleigh." Sebastian had made sure blankets had been tucked into the sleighs.

"Not as long as you hold me close."

"Now that I can do." Putting action to his words, he curled his arm around me and drew me near.

"Better?"

"Much."

For a few moments, we watched the revelers enjoying themselves, laughing, drinking, making jokes.

"Hard to believe we're investigating a murder," I said.

"Life is hard enough. You must find joy where you can."

I glanced up at him. "Are you happy, Robert?"

He tweaked my chin, an endearment of his. "When I'm with you, I am."

"What about when you're not?"

"I count the minutes until I am."

I thought he was making a joke, but he was dead serious. "Kiss me."

He folded me into his arms and pressed his lips to mine

until everything and everyone faded away. It was only him and me in this world of our own creation, being loved, and loving him. After he slowly ended the embrace, I said, "I never imagined it could be like this."

"Like what?"

"Like I would count the world well lost as long as I had you."

He brushed a thumb across my cheek in a tender caress. "You'll always have me, Catherine. And if I have anything to say about it, the world as well."

I rested my hand on his. "Promise?"

He brought my palm to his lips and kissed it. "Promise."

"Hey, you two," My brother Ned's voice. "We're about to make a toast. Join us."

Together, Robert and I joined the guests. The Yule log had been sawed off and secured to a trailer to be hauled back to the castle.

"Sebastian and Margaret," Ned said. "You are purposeful individuals who seek to do the best for others. That will stand you in good stead, as you will think of each other before you think of yourself. You are perfectly suited for each other, and we, your family and friends, wish you nothing but joy and happiness the rest of your lives." Ned raised his glass. "To Sebastian and Margaret."

"To Sebastian and Margaret." Everyone joined the chorus.

"Thank you," Sebastian said, pulling Margaret close to him and dropping a kiss on her head. "It means the world to us that our friends and family," he nodded toward the Worthington clan and his sister, "are here to celebrate with us." Then he blew on his hands. "Now, shall we head back to the castle? It's getting a bit nippy out here."

He had a point. It had grown much colder since our arrival. We piled back into the sleighs, leaving the staff to pack up the food and drink that remained. Once it was brought back to Wynchcombe castle, it would be shared with the staff.

The merriment continued with everyone singing Christmas carols as we traveled through the woods. But our jolly mood did not last long. As soon as we stepped into the castle, we were met by bad news. Mrs. Sweetwater, the castle cook, had become quite ill.

CHAPTER 9

MRS. SWEETWATER

*M*ARGARET, MOTHER, AND I encountered the physician as he was leaving Mrs. Sweetwater's parlor. She was so ill the staff hadn't been able to take her to her bedchamber.

"How is she faring?" Margaret asked.

"Not well. She's suffering from abdominal pain and experiencing numbness and tingling. And her pulse is racing. If I didn't know better, I'd swear she was poisoned."

It seemed my fear had come to pass. Someone had indeed hurt Mrs. Sweetwater. "Did she have anything to eat or drink?"

"Breakfast. But she shared the meal with the rest of the staff, and they're not suffering any symptoms. I was told she drank tea this morning in her parlor while she was working on the menu for the wedding feast. She asked one of the kitchen maids to bring her some hot water, but she used her own special blend."

Alarm bells went off in my head. "It's the tea. Somebody must have put poisonous leaves in the tin. It's the only theory that makes any sense."

The doctor's eyes widened with horror. "Surely not. Who would do such a thing?"

"A murderer. Can you have the tin contents analyzed?"

"Yes, but it will take some time to get back the results. Everyone's on holiday."

"No matter. Take it with you. We'll need to test the container for fingerprints as well, although I suspect the culprit wore gloves."

"What can we do for Mrs. Sweetwater, Doctor?" Margaret asked.

"She'll need to be watched. Around the clock, mind you. I left instructions with Mrs. Branson." He nodded toward the parlor. "She's in there with her now."

"We'll assign four-hour shifts," Margaret said.

"I can help, if you wish," Mother offered.

"No, Mother," Margaret said, pressing Mother's hand. "You've done more than enough. I don't want you to take on this additional task."

"But dear, how will we know who to trust?"

"Have our London staff watch her," I suggested. "They wouldn't have a quarrel with her. Mrs. Simpson can take the first watch. Betsy will be glad to help as well."

"Cummings makes a great nurse," Mother offered.

"Yes, she does." She'd tended to Mother more than once when she'd felt poorly. "She can take the third shift. Grace can take over from her. She's more than proven her worth."

"I agree," Margaret said. "We'll call you, Doctor, if Mrs. Sweetwater takes a turn for the worse."

"Please do. Although I fear there is little I would be able to do. She'll either pull through or she won't. It's in God's hands now. I'll fetch the tin and take it with me."

After he'd done so, and Mother escorted the doctor out, Margaret and I entered Mrs. Sweetwater's parlor. The cot she'd had installed had proved valuable indeed.

"How is she doing, Mrs. Branson?" Margaret asked in a whisper.

"Very poorly, Miss." Her eyes clearly showed how worried she was.

She had good reason to be. Not only was Mrs. Sweetwater deathly pale and sweating profusely, but her breathing was ragged.

"The doctor said not to give her any food or drink and wipe off any vomit which I have done. One of the maids cleaned the room and brought a basin." She wrung her hands. "The bed could use a change of linen, but I fear doing much more."

"The only thing she ate or drank that differed from the staff was the tea?" I asked.

"Yes, Miss. She doesn't store food in here as she fears mice will get to it. If she wishes any, she has it brought around. She didn't do that this morning."

"After she drank her tea, how soon did she grow ill?"

"Almost immediately. She stumbled into the kitchen, spewing vomit. A couple of the kitchen maids and I carried her here. After we put her to bed, I asked them to call the doctor. He arrived about half an hour later. Is she going to recover, Miss?"

"We don't know, Mrs. Branson. All we can do is care for her."

"And pray."

"Yes. And pray."

After Margaret left to arrange the nursing shifts, Mother explained the importance of noting any changes in Mrs. Sweetwater. "If she grows worse, you are to telephone the doctor and alert me."

"Margaret would prefer you get your rest," I reminded her.

"I know, dear. But I couldn't live with myself if this good woman perished while I slept." She turned to Mrs. Branson. "Now, there should be paper and pencil in Mrs. Sweetwater's desk. Everyone who nurses her should write down her observations. Is she pale? Has she slept? Is her skin cold to the touch? That way the next shift nurse will know what to expect."

"If I may, Mrs. Worthington. I've worked at several households. At none of them has the lady of the house taken such care of her staff."

"I know no other way to be, Mrs. Branson."

"Yes, ma'am. Bless you, ma'am."

That night, worried as I was about Mrs. Sweetwater, I tossed and turned in bed. Tomorrow would be another full day, and I needed to get some rest. At home, whenever I couldn't sleep, I'd sneak down to the kitchen and have a glass of milk. Maybe I should do the same.

A glance at my bedside clock told me it was after two. Did I really want to roam through a dark castle at this time of night? For another half hour I tried my best, but sleep eluded me. There really was no choice. I needed to make the trip. And since Mrs. Sweetwater's office was next to the kitchen, I could check on her as well.

Propelling thought to action, I slid into my slippers, wrapped my velvet robe around me, and stepped into the hallway which thankfully was illuminated, although with low lighting. Still, it was better than nothing. I carefully made my way down the staircase as a missed step might send me hurtling toward disaster. After reaching the bottom, I was crossing the Great Hall on the way to the kitchen when the sound of voices reached me. No. Not voices. Only one. Coming from the library. How very curious. Wondering who it could be, I made my way to that room to find . . . no one.

And then I saw her. A lady, a specter really, for she was translucent. Had to be Daisy. She was muttering to herself. "Can't find it."

"What?"

"What I'm looking for. I put it in the cradle, but it's not there. Somebody took it."

The cradle was still in the priest hole. Inspector Fallon had not removed it.

"What are you looking for? Your baby?"

"Yes. No. Something else. He doesn't know who I am." And then she gazed straight at me. "You must find it and give it to him."

"Who?"

"He doesn't know I'm his mother."

"Who? Who doesn't know?"

"My son. You will tell him."

I had to remind myself she was a ghost, most likely a figment of my imagination. The only response I could give was, "Yes. I will."

Suddenly the lights came on in the library. and the specter vanished. "Miss Worthington?"

Mr. Seward. Sebastian's estate manager.

"Yes, it's me."

"Were you looking for something to read?"

"No. Actually I wanted a glass of milk."

"And you thought you'd find it in the library?" His crooked smile teased me. He was quite handsome with his dark hair and bright blue eyes.

"I lost my way."

"It is a big castle. Would you like me to show you the way to the kitchen?"

"Yes, please."

It didn't take long to arrive at the kitchen. True gentleman that he was, he retrieved a jug of milk from an ice box and poured me a glass of milk.

"What were you doing in the library, Mister Seward?"

"I'd been working late and was on the way to my room when I heard voices. Imagine my surprise when I flicked on the lights to find you alone."

I leaned toward him as if I was confiding something. "I'll tell you a little secret, Mr. Seward. When I encounter a problem, I talk to myself. It's something I do to . . . clear the cobwebs, if you will."

Whether out of politeness or sheer amazement, he didn't comment, but the look he sent me spoke volumes.

CHAPTER 10

A WAY OUT

*N*OT ONLY DID MRS. SWEETWATER survive the night, but by midmorning she was eager to leave her sick bed. After the physician examined her, he declared she was out of danger. But he encouraged her to rest one more day. Once she reluctantly agreed, we moved her to her proper bedroom, where she could get a decent sleep. The kitchen maids plied her with tea and broth, all that the doctor would allow her to have. As we had no definite evidence as to who or what had poisoned her, all the food and drink was prepared by Mrs. Branson. We were not taking any chances with Mrs. Sweetwater's health.

Having averted that crisis, Robert and I went exploring. Now that we knew where the other exit to the priest chamber was located, it was only a matter of determining how a person could make their way through it. The wardrobe was too heavy to move, which meant there had to be a way through the furnishing itself.

For a time, we pulled and prodded every inch of the wardrobe until Robert finally figured it out. One of the hooks in the back meant for hanging clothes. He pulled it and, like Aladdin and his magic lamp, the back of the wardrobe dropped down. Behind it was a door. Once I crawled into the wardrobe and slid open its lock, the portal opened away from us. A tunnel similar in size to the one we'd earlier traversed lay in front of us. Unlike the previous one which had been musty in nature, this one contained fresh air. After Robert crawled in after me, we made our way through the labyrinth. Twenty feet into our exploration, the tunnel continued to the right. Farther on, it turned to the left. Finally, we encountered another door secured by a solid brass knob. All we needed to do was turn it. The door opened into a huge bush.

"Where are we?" I asked. We were outside. That was the only thing that was clear.

"Haven't the foggiest. Regardless, let me lead the way."

"Our clothes are going to be ripped and torn. We should have worn something old." Not that I'd brought any. Mother had insisted on an entirely new wardrobe for this trip.

"You stay then," he said. "I'll go."

"I don't think so. Lead on, Macduff."

He grabbed me and kissed me. "Are you always going to use that line?"

"Always." I bussed him back.

"I'll try to keep the worst of the branches off you. Stay close to me."

He didn't have to ask me twice. Any opportunity would do to feel his warmth.

It took him but a few minutes to fight his way to a clearing. In the near distance, cultivated plants grew.

"We're in the back of the castle," I said. "That's the

produce garden." I then pointed to a door to our right. "And that leads to the kitchen."

"It would have been relatively easy for someone to sneak into the castle through that door back there." He pointed toward the way we'd come. "That door was not locked, so they would only need to know of the entrance."

"How? We're the only ones who do."

"We're not the only ones. The murderer does as well. Daisy must have somehow gotten word to him."

"But how did she even find the way out?"

"It could have been accidental. Maybe she was hanging something in the wardrobe, nudged the lever, and the back panel dropped down. She would have made her way out at that point and gone looking for the father of her babe. He would have returned with her so she could show him the way."

I recalled my encounter from the night before. I hadn't told Robert. It'd been so strange. "She would've felt so alone in that room. She would have wanted to reach out to the father of her child, as close as she was to its birth."

"And he betrayed her by killing her. He might even have continued to make his way into the castle after her death."

"With a corpse lying in the priest chamber? That would take someone with a great deal of cold blood."

"Murderers don't have scruples, Catherine. Once he killed Daisy, he wouldn't think twice about it. We should find out if anything's gone missing through the years. Such as the castle silver."

"Good luck trying to find out. Mr. Cogsworth barely knows what day of the week it is."

"You do have a point," he said.

A thought occurred to me. "Maybe that's how he managed to poison Mrs. Sweetwater's tin."

"You don't know that the tin contained poison."

"There's no other explanation, Robert. She certainly would not have poisoned herself. He could have entered late at night when everyone was fast asleep. He'd know the way through the castle because he'd been here before. All he would need to do is nip into the kitchen and drop the poison into the tin. It'd be only a matter of time before Mrs. Sweetwater prepared a cup of tea and died."

"Why would he take such a chance. He'd have to be desperate."

"Because she knows something. Maybe she doesn't remember, or doesn't think it's important. Whatever it is, it threatens him."

"His plan did not succeed."

"Because Mrs. Sweetwater vomited what she'd ingested, and the doctor was brought in right away. If the staff had waited, she might not have survived."

He glanced back toward the way we'd exited. "Sebastian will have to secure that door or build over it."

"As much of a lover of history as Margaret is? I don't think so. They'll probably just put a solid lock on the inside."

I turned toward the door. "Should we go back? It's getting chilly out here."

"Not that way." He removed his jacket and draped it over me. "Let's walk around to the front."

We arrived at the castle gate to discover Lord Newcastle and Lady Wakefield had just arrived and were being properly welcomed in the formal receiving room. They'd traveled from Hertfordshire where Lord Newcastle's country seat was situated along with the cottage where Lady Wakefield and her daughter resided. After her abusive husband had died, she and Lord Newcastle had rekindled their love. As soon as her year of mourning ended, they were planning to wed.

"We were wondering where you'd disappeared to," Sebastian exclaimed. "Come and say hello."

While Lord Newcastle and Robert shook hands, Lady Wakefield and I bussed each other's cheek. But all I could take in was the beautiful dark-haired child next to her. With her periwinkle eyes, she closely resembled her father. "Could this be Lavender Rose?"

"It is. Make your curtsy to Miss Worthington, sweetheart. Show her how much you've learned," Lady Wakefield said, a note of pride in her voice.

"How do you do, Miss Worthington." Lavender Rose sketched a deep curtsy, a challenging thing given she was holding tight to a kitten who appeared none too pleased. "It's a pleasure to see you again."

"Me as well. Is that your kitten?"

"Yes. Her name is Mittens because of her paws." She held the hissing feline up to me. "See. They look like she has gloves." Last time I'd seen her she'd been this silent child who didn't speak a word. Seemingly, that had changed.

"Yes, I see. How very clever of you."

A knock on the door preceded the entrance of a young woman dressed in a grey dress and an apron. "Did you ring for me, Lady Wakefield?"

"I did, Sally. Please show Lavender Rose to her room and accommodate her and Mittens."

Lavender Rose objected. "Mama. I don't wish to go."

Lady Wakefield stroked her daughter's head. "It's been a long day, sweetheart. You'll want to settle into your room. After your bath and supper, I'll come up to say goodnight."

"Promise?"

"Promise."

"And Lord Newcastle too?"

He squatted down to her level. "Me too, Poppet." Anyone

who saw them together would have no trouble determining he was her father as they shared the same coloring.

Taking her nanny's hand, Lavender Rose made her way out of the room, while casting back a sorrowful glance.

"She's beautiful, Lady Wakefield."

"Thank you." She breathed a heavy sigh. "This is her first outing away from home. I fear she may regress."

"To not talking?"

"Yes. She was rather clingy after our arrival. Maybe I should go up to her." She took a step forward, but Lord Newcastle stopped her.

"Best not, dear. Nanny will let us know if she needs you."

"Yes, you're right." But Lady Wakefield couldn't help but cast a worried glance toward the door herself.

CHAPTER 11

DECK THE HALLS

WITH ALL THE EVENTS SURROUNDING THE INVESTIGATION, the Great Hall garlanding had had to wait, but finally it was time. That afternoon, we gathered in that noble space to hang the ivy and holly, light the Yule log, and decorate the twenty-foot Christmas tree. The most excited of all was Lady Lily as that tradition hadn't been observed in all the years she'd lived in the castle. The beautiful frock she was wearing did not hold a candle to her bright smile and the joy on her face.

After the tree had been carried in through the mammoth castle gate, it had been planted in a huge, round metal tub and secured at its top, bottom, and center by strong ropes. No chance it would topple over. Once footmen settled four tall ladders around it, Sebastian explained the rules of the game we were about to play.

As called by Wynchcombe Castle tradition, guests would split up into teams with each one responsible for decorating a section of the tree. To preserve a lady's modesty, gentlemen would station themselves at the top, and ladies would stand toward the bottom. Footmen would hold firm to the ladders to make sure they did not wobble.

"There will be drinking involved," Sebastian said with a grin. "And be warned, we've added rum to the punch."

"Oh, dear," Mother exclaimed.

"To get the game started, I've chosen four captains, one for each team. Mister Worthington will lead one, I will lead another, Lord Newcastle, a third, and Mister Clapham a fourth." And then he named those who would be participating. There was one notable exception.

"What about Robert?" I asked.

"He will act as the referee since he's a Chief Detective Inspector with Scotland Yard, and the only one with a connection to the law."

"Mister Clapham does as well," I pointed out.

"He's retired," Sebastian said. "No offense intended, Mister Clapham."

"None taken, Your Grace," answered Mister Clapham.

"Now, as for the rules," Sebastian continued. If a member of the team breaks a rule, such as not take a drink, Robert will issue a caution. The second time a rule is broken, he will disqualify that person's team."

"That's rather harsh," Marlowe objected. "I mean, what if the lady is a lightweight?"

"Then the lady should pace herself," Lady Lily said.

"Hear, hear," Sebastian said.

Who knew those two were such cutthroats? Usually, they were so mild-mannered.

"Now," Sebastian said. "We'll pick straws to see who chooses team members first. The longest wins, the next longest goes second, and so on."

As luck would have it, Father picked the longest straw. "I

choose my entire family," he said, with a note of pride in his voice. There was only one problem with that statement. The Worthington clan numbered five, one too many. Each team could have only four.

"Thank you, dear Father," Margaret said, "but I'm promised to the Wynchcombe team." She batted her eyelashes at Sebastian who winked at her in return.

"Turncoat," I yelled, good naturally.

"I know which side of my bread is buttered, dear sister." She stuck out her tongue at me.

I reciprocated in kind.

"Girls," Mother chided.

We ceased our hostilities. For the moment.

After Lady Lily was added to Sebastian's group, she yelled, "I choose Hollingsworth."

"Not fair," Lady Emma objected. "The man's a pirate. He'll drink us all under the tree."

Hollingsworth was not a pirate, simply a seafaring man, not that there was a smidgen of difference when it came to imbibing alcohol. Or so I believed.

"*He* won't be drinking," Sebastian said, an amused grin on his lips.

"I won't?" Hollingsworth seemed disappointed.

"No. As the gentlemen will be at the top of the ladder, we can't risk a fall. They will remain sober. The ladies will be the ones drinking."

"Point of order, Your Grace," Lady Carlyle said. "What if a lady objects?"

"Then her team will forfeit."

Lady Emma gave her mother a pointed glare. "You will do this, Mother. I know things." Blatant blackmail on Lady Emma's part. Good for her.

"Very well," Lady Carlyle said with a sniff. She did not appear pleased.

Sebastian continued with his explanation of the rules. "The lady on the ground will be responsible for handing the decorations to the lady on the ladder. She will need to drink a thimbleful of punch before she hands off each one," Sebastian said. "So will the lady higher up."

"Well, that shouldn't be a problem," Mother said, visibly relieved.

"This is one of the thimbles." He held one up. The thing was five times the usual size.

Mother tensed once more. "Oh, oh, dear."

"Maybe I should be the one at the bottom," I suggested.

"I don't fare well with heights, Kitty. Besides, you'll have to drink as well."

She did have a point.

By the end of the choosing, Lord Newcastle's team included Lady Wakefield, Lord Marlowe, and Lady Emma. Mister Clapham's was made up of Lady Carlyle, Lady Melissande, and Sebastian's Oxford friend, William Darrow. His sister, Eliza, had retired to her room as she wasn't feeling well.

"Any questions before we begin?"

"How many decorations are there?" Lady Melissande asked.

"Thirty in all."

"What if someone drops one?" Lady Emma asked.

"It will be replaced. We have plenty more." He pointed to a box filled to the brim. "Now footmen will hand the thimbleful of punch to the lady on the ground. Once she has drunk it, a maid will hand her the first decoration which she will then pass to the next person who will also need to drink a thimbleful. You'll need to ensure the decorations are evenly disbursed—ten at the top, ten in the middle, ten at the bottom. The first team to hang all its decorations wins."

"What's the bloody prize?" Marlowe asked.

"Lord Marlowe! Language," Mother admonished.

"Begging your pardon, ma'am." It wasn't the first time he'd been chastised by mother, nor I dared say would it be the last.

"Any more questions?"

No one breathed so much as a word.

After everyone had stationed themselves, either on the ladder, or on the ground, Sebastian yelled from his great height at the top of his ladder, "Inspector Crawford, if you will start us off."

He was referring to him now as Inspector Crawford whereas before he'd called him Robert. Probably to imbue him with the authority befitting his role.

"Ready?" Robert yelled.

Everyone nodded.

"Go!"

The first thimbleful was handed to Mother who gamely drank it. A ribbon was handed to her by one of the maids. I'd already drunk my thimbleful so all I had to do was pass the ribbon to Ned and he, in turn, hand it to Father.

"Well, that wasn't too—"

"Mother, pass me an ornament."

After taking another swallow of the punch, she did just that. But then, she paused. "Edward that ribbon is crooked."

"It just needs to be hanged, Mildred. Doesn't matter what it looks like."

"It matters to me. I have some pride, you know."

We were going to lose. "Mother, step up the pace."

"Yes, dear."

The next twenty minutes were sheer chaos. Cries of "You dropped the ribbon, you oaf," from Lady Emma. No clue to whom it had been directed. More than likely, Lord Marlowe.

I took a ribbon from Mother and tied it to the tree.

"Ahem," Robert said. "That will be a demerit for team Worthington."

I twisted toward him. "What?"

"You did not take a drink."

"I didn't pass the bag of nuts. You only must drink if you hand it off."

"Everyone stop," Robert yelled.

All froze.

"Point of clarification. Sebastian, do you need to drink even if you don't pass the decoration?"

"Yes," the traitor said with a devilish grin.

"The demerit for team Worthington stands."

I glared at him from my perch. He would pay for that.

"Carry on," he yelled, winking at me.

The troll!

In the end, we didn't come in last. That honor belonged to Lord Newcastle's group, the infighting between Marlowe and Lady Emma caused them the loss. The winner was Mister Clapham's team who'd worked together in unison without any strife. With much fanfare, Sebastian awarded a trophy to every member of that team, and then we all stood back to gaze at our handiwork.

"That's the worst decorated Christmas tree I've ever seen," Lord Marlowe declared with a sneer to his lips.

He had a point. In one section, ribbons were bunched up together, while in another ornaments hanged willy-nilly among rows of fruits, nuts, cranberries, and the occasional paper ornament. Entire areas lacked any decoration at all.

"Well, I think it's beautiful," Lady Lily said, tears in her eyes. "I hope we do it again and again for years to come."

Sebastian gave her a brotherly hug. "I agree, and we will." Margaret stepped to his other side and curled an arm around his waist. All three gazed at the tree, a look of wonder in their eyes.

"Now, let's stop all this foolish sentiment," Sebastian said after a moment or two. Never mind his own eyes had grown rather moist. "Let's light the Yule log." With much fanfare, the log was set ablaze. No chance the tree would catch fire as it had been situated a safe distance away. Still, they placed a huge screen in front of the mammoth fireplace to keep sparks from flying out.

While some of the footmen carried away the ladders and the boxes of extra decorations, others brought in more food and drink. Sebastian had arranged for a quintet of musicians to play music. Soon, we were not only eating and drinking but dancing as well.

The first tune was a country reel. The only ones who knew most of the steps were Mother, and of all people, Mister Clapham. But then they were both raised in the country, so it made sense. The rest of us joined in as best we could, laughing when we turned the wrong way, and falling into each other's arms when we did.

The evening ended with everyone singing Christmas carols—*While Shepherds Watched their Flocks by Night*, *God Rest Ye Merry, Gentlemen*, *Greensleeves*, my favorite, and many others. The celebration ended when the guests, claiming exhaustion, said goodnight. There were plenty of sore feet tonight, and I imagined, sore heads in the morning; but everyone went to bed with a glad heart.

I, however, had no wish to lay down my head. At least not yet. Needing something more, I asked Robert if we could venture outside. While we'd been enjoying the festivities, it had begun to snow, turning the castle grounds into a winter wonderland. After we walked a fair distance down the road that led away from the castle, we turned to gaze back at it.

Gorgeous did not begin to describe it. "How beautiful."

"Would you like to live in one? Or a smaller version at least?"

I turned into him, seeking his warmth. "Imagine the upkeep." I only half faked my shudder since the temperature was downright frigid. "I much prefer the coziness of your Eaton Square home, especially the library."

"You haven't seen my bedroom yet," he murmured.

Laughing, I gazed up at him. "Is that an offer to show it to me?"

"Once we're married, I will."

I swatted his chest. "You horrible man. Why tease me like that?"

"Because I love to hear you laugh."

I curled my arms around his neck and drew him to me. "Kiss me, Inspector."

"With pleasure, Miss Worthington."

His lips were warm as they pressed against me, stealing my breath away. While snowflakes danced around us, landing occasionally on my head, I got lost in the wonder of his warm embrace.

"Ummm," I murmured once he ended the kiss.

Gazing off into the horizon, he said, "We should head back. The snow is getting heavier."

I would have loved to stay in this magical place, so full of Christmas promise, but he was right.

As neither of us wished the magic to end, we did not hurry, but took our time enjoying the falling snow and wondrous sights along the way. But eventually, we made it once more inside.

A footman was stationed by the entrance waiting to take our outer garments.

"Thank you, Joseph." He was a strapping young man, one of the new hires. "Hope we didn't keep you waiting too long."

"Not at all, Miss. It's my responsibility to lock up the castle for the night."

"And a great big responsibility it is. Good night."

"Goodnight, Miss. Sir." Putting words to action, he dropped the great big bar across the castle gate. No way could someone break through it, not as thick as it was.

Before we made our way up the stairs, Robert and I paused at the Great Hall to watch the Yule log burn in the fireplace.

"Tonight was quite wonderful, wasn't it?" I asked. "Such a joyous celebration with family and friends."

"That's what Christmas is all about. Family, friends, food. Goodwill toward men."

"And women."

"And women." He dropped a kiss on my head. "And the hope of a bright future."

He escorted me up the stairs to my door where we kissed again.

"Someday, we won't have to say goodnight anymore," I murmured.

He cupped my cheek. "You have only to name the date, my darling."

I breathed out a sigh. I wasn't quite ready to do that. "I love you, Robert."

"And I adore you, Catherine."

I don't know how long we would have stayed there saying goodnight if a door hadn't creaked open nearby. Alerted to the sound, we turned in its direction, a room two doors down. We watched in fascination as Marlowe emerged, half dressed, shirt open, jacket and waistcoat draped over one arm, shoes and socks held in his other hand.

"Evening," he said as nonchalantly as you please while he continued his march down the hall toward the wing the gentlemen occupied.

"Heavens!" I said.

"Indeed," Robert replied.

CHAPTER 12

THE MORNING AFTER

$\mathcal{A}$ NXIOUS AS I WAS to talk to Lady Emma the following morning, I had to force myself to wait until a reasonable time. She was neither an early riser, not a late one. So, I deemed ten would be the most propitious time. When the clock struck the hour, I headed down the stairs, hoping she'd be in the dining room. Thankfully, she was there, the only guest in the room, calmly buttering a piece of toast.

"Good morning," I said.

"And good morning to you."

After I piled eggs, bacon, baked beans, tomatoes, and mushrooms on my plate, I joined her at the table. When one of the footmen in the room asked what I'd like to drink, I indicated coffee which he poured for me.

Searching for a conversation starter, I settled on, "Did you enjoy last night?"

"Yes, indeed." An amused smile accompanied that statement.

"Robert and I ventured outside after the celebration ended."

"Did you?" She crunched down on the toast.

"Yes. When we returned, he escorted me to my room. We were saying our goodnights when someone emerged from a room two doors down."

"Well, don't keep me in suspense."

"Lord Marlowe," I whispered since I didn't wish the footmen to overhear.

"Heavens. Was he visiting a lady?"

"Yes. You."

"Are you sure? It could have been Mother." While I felt the need to whisper, she had no such compunction.

"As if he would ever be caught in her room. What on earth were you thinking?" I hissed. "If your mother had seen him, she would have you engaged in a thrice and an engagement announcement sent to *The Times* the same day."

"Really, Kitty. I don't know if you saw her, but Mother had a bit to drink last night. She wouldn't have noticed a herd of elephants tromping through her room. I doubt she'll rise before noon."

"But—"

"Kitty, dear." She calmly sipped her tea. "I love you like a sister, but what that particular gentleman and I do is our business." At least, she'd whispered that last part.

"I don't want you to get hurt."

"Trust me. I know what I'm doing."

"Very well." I straightened my serviette. "I apologize if I stepped out of line."

She patted my hand. "No need. I know you have only the best intentions."

Lady Lily breezed in, a smile on her face, precluding any further discussion. "Good morning."

After we responded in kind, she filled her plate and joined us at the table.

"Any plans for the guests today?" I asked. If there were, I would need to adjust my own.

"None. After yesterday, Sebastian figured we'd all need a day of rest. So do whatever pleases you."

"Speaking of gentlemen, where are they?" None were present at the table. I turned toward one of the footmen. "Have they already broken their fast?"

"They breakfasted early, Miss, before heading out."

"All of them?"

"Yes, Miss."

"That's odd, don't you think?" I asked Lady Emma.

"Maybe they went on a shooting spree."

"In the dearth of winter? In case you haven't noticed, it snowed last night. Doubt there are any birds on the trees."

"They could be hunting small game—rabbits and such."

"Oh, please don't say so." I couldn't bear the thought of some woodland creature being shot, skinned, braised in a sauce, and served at the dinner table.

"Miss Worthington," a footman said over my shoulder. "Excuse me for interrupting. Mister Clapham left this for you." He handed me a note.

"Oh?" I opened the envelope to learn he'd received word last night about a possible lead and had gone to Yorkshire to follow it.

"What does it say?" Lady Emma asked.

I didn't want the footmen to hear this particular conversation. "Best discuss it in my parlor. Meet me there in an hour?"

"Of course."

"What about you, Kitty? Are you scheduling another meeting?" Lady Lily asked.

"Not today. I have other matters to attend to."

Within a short while, the other ladies streamed in. After spending a few convivial minutes with them, I excused myself and headed for the kitchen, as I wanted to talk to Mrs. Sweetwater. Not only did I wish to check on her health, but I had more questions for her.

As Sir Winston was there happily ensconced in a spot sure to be the warmest in the room, I stopped to say hello. "I hope he's no bother," I said to those in the room.

"On the contrary," Mrs. Branson said, "we love to have him. He's a friendly sort. Always happy for a pat on the head."

"And the occasional sausage or two." Our Worthington House cook, Mrs. Cutler, said. She knew of Sir Winston's predilection for that particular fare.

"He's mad about them."

While Mrs. Sweetwater recuperated, Mrs. Branson and Mrs. Butler were doing most of the food preparation.

"I'd like a word with Mrs. Sweetwater. Do you know where she is?"

"In her parlor."

"Thank you." After a quick knock on that door, I entered to find Mrs. Sweetwater quite recovered. Her cheeks were no longer pasty white but bloomed with color, and her eyes were shiny and bright.

She greeted me with a smile. "Miss Worthington, what a pleasure. Please take a seat."

"Thank you, Mrs. Sweetwater. Are you feeling better?"

"Much. They won't let me do much, you know. So, I'm resting, but I'll be back up to full strength on Christmas Eve. Nothing is going to keep me from preparing that meal."

"I'm so glad."

"What can I do for you?"

84

"If you're up to it, I have some questions about the day you became ill."

"I was poisoned, Miss Worthington. I know that now."

"Did anyone step into your office that day?"

"No one except the lass who brought me hot water for me tea."

"Did you have a biscuit?"

"No. I had nothing to eat. The doctor mentioned he was testing the leaves in my tea tin. He thinks that's where the poison was."

"Yes, we discussed that the day you became ill. Can you think of anyone who would want to hurt you?"

"No, Miss." She straightened up. "I have no enemies either in the kitchen or among the castle staff. We all get along. No one here would wish me such harm, much less act upon it."

"What about the recent hires? Anyone who wished you ill."

"I don't see how, Miss. I barely know most of them. They seem happy enough to be putting in an honest day's work for good wages."

I had to concur with that statement, as I had helped Mother and Margaret with the interviews. All had been eager to work at the castle and earn a generous pay. True, a devious person would know how to make himself agreeable for the short amount of time we'd talked to him. But surely, we would have heard by now if a person was not who he, or she, seemed. As far as I knew, there had been neither comments nor complaints. I would need to pursue another tack.

I glanced down at my journal where I'd written my questions. "Could someone have gotten into this room without your knowledge?"

"I don't see how. I lock it whenever I leave the room. I have cash in here, you see. Although Mr. Seward pays all the accounts, we occasionally have a delivery that requires immediate payment in cash."

"I see. Well, thank you, Mrs. Sweetwater."

"Are you still investigating Daisy's murder?"

I nodded. "Yes, we are."

"Better you than Inspector Fallon. He was never any good as a constable. I expect he's not any good as an inspector, either."

That was a surprise to me. "Inspector Fallon was a constable?"

"Yes. About twenty-five, thirty years ago."

"Around the time Daisy died?"

"Before then."

"Was she sweet on him?"

She laughed. "If she was, he wouldn't have given her the time of day. He was a handsome gentleman. Still is, for that matter. All the lasses were in love with him. Not sure if it was the uniform or him. But he had his eye on Mister Allston's daughter, Clara. The man owned half the businesses in Headbourne Worthy, and plenty more in Winchester."

Well, that was interesting, very interesting indeed.

"Constable Fallon was an ambitious man, you see, and Mister Allston had enough influence to get him promoted to detective inspector. So, he got Miss Alston to marry him. Against her father's wishes, I'll have you know. He'd taken the measure of the man and found him wanting. But Clara was his only child and he wanted her to be happy. So, he accepted the marriage and put in a word with the Winchester Constabulary. Eventually, Constable Fallon became a detective inspector."

"Was the marriage successful?"

"For a time, it was. She gave him two daughters, but what he really wanted was a son. She died in childbirth on her fourth attempt. Maybe ten years after they wed. His father-in-law blamed him for his daughter's death and withdrew his support. So, detective inspector was as high as he got."

Inspector Fallon's reluctance to investigate Daisy's murder now loomed large. He did have a valid argument, though. Very little could be accomplished during the Christmas holiday. But was it more than that? Could he in fact be the murderer? One of the sewing circle ladies had mentioned a constable who'd been sweet on Daisy. But she'd said the name was Clemson. The names did not match. "Was there a Constable Clemson in the village at one time?"

"Oh, yes, indeed there was. Now, he was sweet on Daisy. He died shortly after her disappearance."

So there had been two of them. Maybe the niece who explained it to Lady Emma got the names wrong. But since the aunt had passed away, there was no way to clarify it. And with the wedding two days away, time was running out. Hopefully, Mister Clapham would return with news about where John Stirling had gone. He could very well hold the key to solving this mystery.

CHAPTER 13

EXPLORATION

*A*FTER I THANKED MRS. SWEETWATER for her time, I stepped into the kitchen where Sir Winston was being fed a sausage. That's when I noticed something odd about him.

"He's limping."

"Yes, poor mite," Mrs. Branson said as she rolled out a pastry. "He stepped on a pinecone when a footman took him for one of his walks. The stable master put a salve on his paw. He should be right as rain by the wedding day."

I leaned down to pat his head. "Oh, Sir Winston, I'm so sorry. You must take care where you step now that you're in the country."

"Woof!" He gazed at me with sorrowful eyes.

"I'll let Father know so he can visit. That should make you feel better." Father was definitely Sir Winston's favorite.

"Woof! Woof!"

"Oh, he's already been," Mrs. Branson said. "Fed him those sausages himself."

Figured. Father could never stop himself from giving Sir Winston the food he dearly loved.

I returned to my parlor to jot down my observations about my conversation with Mrs. Sweetwater. Since I was expecting, Lady Emma, I'd left the door open. But it was Lord Marlowe who stopped by.

"You wouldn't happen to know the way to the kitchen?" He was a sight to behold. Not only were his clothes rumpled, but a purple bruise had materialized over his half-closed right eye.

"What on earth happened to you?" I asked in horror.

"I ran into Wynchcombe's fist."

"Sebastian hit you? Why?"

"He saw me last night sneaking back into my room and correctly deduced where I'd been. So, given none of Lady Emma's brothers are present, he took it upon himself to defend her honor."

"By hitting you? Since when is anything resolved with a round of fisticuffs?"

He shrugged. "I'm just glad no blood was shed. In the last century, it would have been a duel."

"You do have a point. Er, about last night."

"I would be immensely grateful if you suffered a memory lapse regarding what you saw."

"I'm sorry. I can't. Lady Emma is my friend." She'd specifically asked me to stay out of her affairs. But it was something I simply couldn't do.

He gazed down at the ground. "'Twas dashing embarrassing, if you have to know."

That was a rather odd statement. "What was?"

"Last night. Here I am an expert at whist and am roundly

beaten by a lady. I couldn't hold up my head at my club if they knew."

"I'm sorry. Am I to understand you were playing cards last night in Lady Emma's room?"

"Yes."

"But you emerged half dressed."

"Well, dash it all, we couldn't very well play for money, Lady Emma being not quite as flush as she would need to be. So, she suggested we play for our garments."

"*She* suggested?"

"Yes."

"And you agreed?"

He frowned as if he found my intellect lacking. "Of course. It was the gentlemanly thing to do."

"So how exactly did this work?"

"Every time one of us lost a point, some article of clothing would be removed."

"All you had on were trousers. How much clothing did Lady Emma lose?"

"A handkerchief and a head ribbon. I've never seen a finer player in all my born days."

"And you?"

"You saw me, Miss Worthington, I was practically bare as the day I was born. My trousers would have been next. So, being a gentleman, I forfeited the game."

"Did you explain this to Sebastian?"

His eyes grew wide with outrage. Well, one of them anyway. "Of course not! He would have laughed his head off. Now which way is the kitchen? I need a beefsteak to put on my eye."

After I pointed him in the right direction, he gathered the dignity he had left and proceeded down the hallway.

I'd kept my amusement to myself while he'd been present. But once he was gone, I couldn't hold it in any longer. That's how Lady Emma found me, howling with laughter.

"What's so hilarious?" She asked a wrinkle to her brow.

"Close the door."

"Well," she said once she'd done so.

"Last night. You and Marlowe." I could barely get the words out I was laughing so hard.

All knitted brow, she propped her fists on her hips. "How did you find out?"

"From him. He was wandering around looking for the kitchen."

"Whyever was he doing that?"

"To find a beefsteak to put over his eye. He has quite the shiner. Sebastian gave it to him defending your honor."

"Oh, for the love of—" She raced out of the room, no doubt headed for the kitchen.

A few minutes later Robert found me still convulsed with laughter.

"What's so amusing?"

I sobered up in a hurry. "Did you participate in this morning's demonstration of sheer male stupidity?"

"Found out, did you?" He asked, a grin on his face.

"Obviously."

"I tried to dissuade them from it. Not that it did any good. After Sebastian challenged Marlowe, claiming a lady's honor had to be satisfied, Marlowe couldn't back down. So, I went along to make sure they would not pummel each other. If either got seriously hurt, it most surely ruin your sister's wedding."

"Well, thank you for that. I saw Marlowe. Was Sebastian similarly hurt?"

"No. Marlowe kept it to body blows. So did Sebastian, for that matter. The only reason Marlowe ended up with a shiner is because the idiot dodged low."

"Men!"

"Indeed."

"While the gentlemen were making idiots of themselves, I've been carrying on with the investigation. We need to visit the priest chamber. There's something I need to explore."

He patted his chest. "I have my torch."

"Good. We'll need it."

Unfortunately, the cradle did not reveal any secrets. Neither did the bed, the mattress, the wardrobe, or any other piece of furniture in the room.

"I was so sure we'd find something."

"Such as?"

"Something pointing to the identity of her murderer. Daisy came to me in the library, Robert."

He raised a brow. "Did she?"

"Three nights ago. She said I should look in the cradle. That was the place she hid it."

"Hid what?"

"She didn't say. But it must be the proof, don't you think?"

"Maybe." Doubt was written all over his face.

"You think she was a figment of my imagination."

"I think you've been working too hard."

"Please don't patronize me."

"I'm not." He stepped up to me and gently braced my shoulders. "Tell you what. Let's go for a sleigh ride. The sun's shining. It's beautiful out there."

"I suppose there's nothing much we can do until Mister Clapham returns."

His brow wrinkled. "Where did he go?"

"Yorkshire. He got a message last night. Hopefully, with a lead to John Stirling's whereabouts. While we're on that sleigh ride, I'll tell you all about what Mrs. Sweetwater said."

CHAPTER 14

WEDDING DAY

*A*S MARLOWE COULDN'T VERY WELL hide the bruise on his face, he'd devised a tale. After having a bit too much to drink the night before, he'd missed a step and landed on his face. Regardless of what everyone privately thought, they all commiserated and wished him speedy healing.

The next day saw the arrival of Pastor Pennyworth, his wife, Eleanor, affectionately called Bumble, and their precious five-month old, Ophelia. They were sorry Mister Clapham was not present but were warmly welcomed into the fold. Lord Rutledge, the last of the guests, was also scheduled to reach Wynchcombe Castle that evening as he was catching a later train.

It being the day before the wedding, which was to be held on Christmas Eve, the only event worth of note was the wedding rehearsal. Both Lady Lily and I would be attending to Margaret. So would Lavender Rose who would carry a small basket of flowers. Ned and Robert were to be ushers while Sebastian's friend from Oxford, Mister Darrow, would act as the groomsman.

After the wedding rehearsal, the gentlemen whisked Sebastian to Headbourne Worthy to hold the stag party at the pub. We ladies held a more modest hen do in the conservatory, which Sebastian had decorated with some of the gorgeous flowers and exotic plants he'd grown in the estate greenhouses.

The next day dawned cold but clear. As the wedding ceremony would not be held until four, we spent the morning riddled with nerves. Since it was bad form for the groom to see his bride, we'd scheduled breakfast for the ladies at ten, and the gentlemen at eleven. Bathing and dressing took up the early afternoon. But by three, we were dressed, coiffed, and perfumed.

Margaret's gown had been fashioned from silk with a cross-over bodice and a gathered sash on the hip. Her head was adorned with a pearl cap from which a long lace-trimmed veil flowed. Pearl buckled white satin shoes completed her ensemble. Mother had chosen to wear a black frock with a handkerchief hem and a lace flounce and matching cuffs. Lady Lily and I wore gowns similar in style to Margaret's but pink in color. When Margaret emerged from her room into the hallway, there wasn't a dry eye amongst us, including Father's.

Holding tight to his arm, Margaret made her way down the stairs to the oohs and aahs of the staff who'd gathered at the bottom. As she walked by, every one of them showered blessings upon her.

Finally, after all these months, the moment was here. She would walk down the aisle as Margaret Worthington and return as the Duchess of Wynchcombe. The organ struck the opening chords to *Canon* by Pachebel, and everyone came to their feet. The wedding party made their way down the aisle, Margaret and Father in front, the attendants in the back. Lavender Rose dropped her flower basket only once. To everyone's delight, she yelled "Whoopsie-daisy," picked it up, and continued her walk as if this was something she did every day of the week.

As is tradition, Sebastian did not turn around but waited until Margaret stood next to him to gaze at her. The look he gave her, filled with such wonder and love, was something I would never forget.

Lady Lily and I took our seats on the left side's front row while Robert and Ned, who'd performed ushering duties, did the same on the right.

The wedding ceremony did not take long, as such was Sebastian's and Margaret's wish. After Pastor Pennyworth declared Sebastian and Margaret man and wife, they made their way to the vestry to sign the marriage documents. The wait provided everyone with the opportunity to observe the beauty of the chapel. Built in the sixteenth century and added to in later years, it contained stained glass windows through which the sun streamed, shedding colored lights on one side of the chapel.

A nativity set had been erected to right, complete with statues of Mary and Joseph, and angels and shepherds. The only figure missing was that of the baby Jesus which would not make its appearance until the stroke of midnight.

When Margaret and Sebastian emerged from the vestry, the radiance of their joy rivaled the glow from the sun. They slowly proceeded up the aisle to Mendelssohn's *Wedding March* while everyone showered good wishes upon them.

The Great Hall had been splendidly decorated. Not only did it contain the abominably ornamented Christmas tree but holly and ivy had been hanged in every corner of the room. Buckets and buckets of roses, lilies, and chrysanthemums—Margaret's, Lady Lily's, and Mother's favorite flowers—adorned the room. The banquet tables fairly groaned with food and drink.

Sebastian and Margaret took their places at the head table, with Mother, Father, Ned, and me on one side. And Lady Lily, Mister Darrow, and Lord Rutledge on the other. The rest of the guests were spread out along the tables on both sides of the room.

The place settings consisted of a gold charger with a vintage red and gold dinner set and gold flatware. The wine goblets had been crafted from pure gold and studded with gemstones.

After footmen filled every goblet with wine, Sebastian came to his feet and raised his glass.

"To my wife, Margaret, the new Duchess of Wynchcombe. Today we've been united in holy matrimony by God's representative on earth. You are the shining light in my life. I hope and pray we will have a bright future filled with laughter and joy."

"And male children!" Marlowe yelled. "An heir and a spare at least."

Sebastian waved him down. "Cease, peasant, or I shall toss you into the dungeon!"

Everyone laughed, including Marlowe.

It seemed they'd settled their differences.

"Now what was I saying?" Sebastian asked.

"Bright future, laughter, and joy," Margaret reminded him.

He captured her hand and kissed it. "I surely do adore you, my dearest love." Raising his goblet once more, he exclaimed, "To Margaret, the Duchess of Wynchcombe. My wife."

Everyone raised their goblets. "To Margaret."

"Now, let us eat, drink, and be merry," Sebastian said, "and help us celebrate our joyous day."

As that was the signal to serve the wedding feast, a line of footmen entered the Great Hall carrying the first course—hearty bowls of potage—which they placed in front of every guest. Everyone hungrily ate every spoonful, for breakfast had been hours ago. Once that was consumed, the footmen once again made an appearance. This time carrying platters of salmon and scallops which made up the fish course. That was followed by crown roast beef, accompanied by roasted potatoes and green beans. Dessert consisted of custard, dates drizzled with honey, and spiced pears poached with mead. By the end of the meal, I doubted I could move. Medieval feasts were clearly not for the faint of stomach.

But the celebration was just beginning. Musicians, who'd been stationed in the minstrel's gallery above the Great Hall, struck up a tune, and the dancing began. Sebastian had chosen a waltz for his and Margaret's first dance. After a couple of turns about the space, he encouraged everyone to join in.

Bowing before me, Robert held out his hand. "Would you care to dance, Miss Worthington?"

I grinned at him. "With pleasure, Inspector."

Others paired up, Mother and Father, Lily and Ned, Lady Wakefield and Lord Newcastle. That couple became a trio as they included Lavender Rose who was beaming for all she was worth. Lord Rutledge danced with Lady Wakefield, Lady Melissande with Mr. Darrow, and Lord Hollingsworth with Eliza Darrow. As the evening progressed and more toasts were offered, everyone's spirits rose.

But it had been a long day, and soon the older generation deemed it time to seek their rest. Lord Rutledge and Lady Carlyle went off by their lonesome. Father and Mother, after kissing Margaret goodnight and embracing Sebastian, said their goodnights. Lady Wakefield and Lord Newcastle did the same but, of course, to separate chambers. The younger members of the wedding party remained, but not for long. When the clock in the Great Hall struck eleven, Sebastian and Margaret, arm in arm, quietly disappeared up the stairs.

"They're very well matched," Robert whispered into my ear. "And should enjoy a long and happy life."

"I certainly wish that for them and more."

He gazed around the Great Hall which at this point contained only the Darrows and us. "Lady Emma and Lord Marlowe have gone missing."

"Maybe they're playing whist again."

His mouth quirked up with mirth. "Is that what they were doing last night?"

"You didn't hear it from me. If Lady Emma is fortunate, maybe this time she'll manage to lose."

"Don't you mean the opposite?"

"Not in this case." I curled my arm around his elbow. "Now that's enough talk about them. Shall we head over to the solarium. With all that glass, we can watch the stars."

He hitched up an amused brow. "It's quite cloudy tonight. You won't be able to see a single one."

I tossed him a saucy smile. "Well, then, we'll just have to find something else to do."

CHAPTER 15

CHRISTMAS DAY

*A*FTER THE WEDDING DAY FESTIVITIES, everyone was rightfully exhausted. Since breakfast wouldn't be served in the main dining room until ten, everyone took the opportunity to sleep late. But Grace was kind enough to bring me a pot of coffee to start the day.

"It's lovely out, Miss," she said, drawing the curtains open.

Rising from bed, I walked to the window. The sun shone brightly on a snowy landscape below. "What a perfect Christmas morning."

After bathing and dressing in a red velvet gown with a white fur-edged collar, and a white low-waist silk sash from which matching ribbons flowed, I descended the stairs to find several guests in the dining room tucking into their plates.

"Happy Christmas morning!" I exclaimed.

The greeting was joyously returned, clearly by some,

mumbled by others who happened to be caught with a spoonful of food in their mouths.

The breakfast menu consisted of the usual sausage and bacon, potatoes, tomatoes, and baked beans as well as sumptuous Christmas fare—Bloody Mary scrambled eggs, smoked salmon, a ham and sausage casserole, crumpets with burnt honey butter, and spiced bread. The warm porridge, with its plum, raisin, and granola topper, was especially appreciated this cold Christmas morn.

Christmas Day service was at noon which was presided over by Pastor Pennyworth. He preached love and joy, happiness and goodwill toward men. The baby Jesus had made his appearance in the creche watched over by Mary and Joseph, with the three wise men delivering their gifts.

After Christmas service, we entertained ourselves in different parts of the castle until two o'clock. That's when the Headbourne Worthy residents were due to arrive. In the midst of that celebration, Mister Clapham finally returned. His daughter, Bumble ran to him holding baby Ophelia in her arms while Pastor Pennyworth followed in a more leisurely pace. After we welcomed him and wished him a Happy Christmas, he introduced the man standing next to him. John Stirling, the former footman at Wynchcombe Castle. If there was any doubt as to his identity, it roundly vanished when Mrs. Sweetwater greeted him warmly. The question in all of our minds was, of course, what had happened to Daisy's child. Well, that question was soon answered by the unlikeliest of individuals.

"Uncle John!" Mister Seward exclaimed.

"My dear nephew." Tears streamed down Mister Stirling's face as they greeted each other with a warm embrace.

"I'm so glad you're here," Mister Seward said. "But I don't understand. Did His Grace invite you?" he asked glancing back toward Sebastian.

"If I'd known, I certainly would have," Sebastian replied. "But I did not."

"Then who?"

"I'm responsible for his presence," Mister Clapham said, stepping forward.

"I thank you, Sir, from the bottom of my heart." Mister Seward said, shaking his hand. "It makes my Christmas Day celebration complete."

"Jack," Mister Stirling said, "there's something I must tell you. Is there somewhere private we can go?"

"Yes, of course. My study," Mister Seward said, glancing back at Sebastian. "If I may, Your Grace?"

"Go," Sebastian answered.

They were not the only ones who needed privacy. Mister Clapham requested the same so he could explain what he'd found. Robert and I led him to the parlor Margaret had provided for me.

"Mister Stirling, of course, is the footman who took away Daisy's babe," Mister Clapham said. "He fled in the night with the mite in his arms. Once he reached Headbourne Worthy, he approached the woman who'd lost her own child. She accepted his offer for she had no reason to say. The next day, they left for King's Worth where Mister Stirling's family reluctantly took them in. Apparently, he explained he was the child's father. As soon as the babe was weaned, John, the babe, and the woman traveled to Yorkshire. That's where the woman was from. Her family welcomed them with open arms, and John Stirling set about raising the child on his own. He proved to be a bright lad and eventually made his way to London where he was hired by—"

"Worthington & Son," I said.

"Exactly."

"And when Sebastian needed a man of business," I said,

"Ned recommended him. He came to work at Wynchcombe Castle with no idea this is where he was born."

"What a wondrous tale," Robert said.

"It's not a tale. It's the truth," I said. "Does he know who Mister Seward's father is?"

"Inspector Fallon. Daisy told him the night her child was born. She had evidence, a letter Fallon wrote to her admitting the parentage which she showed to John Stirling. She must have hidden it somewhere in the priest chamber."

"It's not there,"Robert said. "We looked."

"Somewhere else in the castle then," Mister Clapham said.

"But where?"

Suddenly I remembered what Daisy had told me. "The cradle."

"We looked, Catherine," Robert reminded me again.

I shook my head. "It was Christmas. She wanted to keep it somewhere safe, somewhere no one would look for it."

"And what place is that?"

"The nativity scene. She told me, Robert. She told me to look in the cradle. It was baby Jesus's cradle she was talking about."

His eyes widened. "Let's go look."

The three of us raced out of the parlor and headed for the chapel. I prayed as hard as I could the entire way. We arrived to find an empty chapel. Thank heaven. I don't know how we would have explained what we were about to do. I carefully lifted the baby Jesus statue from the creche and handed it to Robert who carefully cradled the figure in his arms. I sent him a fond look. He would make a wonderful father someday.

I passed the swaddling, the pillow, and the fresh straw to Mister Clapham. Nothing was left but the cradle itself which was built from wood. A close inspection revealed nothing.

"It's not here. I was so sure." I said, full disappointment in my voice.

"Here. You take the baby." Robert handed it to me.

He turned the cradle upside down and examined it carefully. There was no place a letter could be hidden.

"Ahem," Mister Clapham said.

"Yes?"

"Look at the pillow."

"Oh!" I said handing the baby back to Robert. The pillow had been fashioned from silk satin and braided in gold. But one edge of the braid seemed loose. While most of the braid had been expertly stitched, one part had received a rather shoddy treatment. "I'll have to rip it apart."

"I'm sure Sebastian won't mind," Robert said. He reached into his coat pocket and retrieved a small Swiss army knife.

I bit back a smile. "Is there anything you don't carry on you, Inspector?"

"I believe in being prepared, Miss Worthington."

I did try to be careful, but it was no use. The braid came apart in my hand. Once that was done, it was an easy matter to rip open the seam that held the pillow together. Taking a deep breath, I rummaged within. Something shaped like an envelope crinkled. I slowly retrieved it and held it on my hand. The envelope, made from cheap paper, had been opened once upon a time. As gently as I could, I retrieved its content. A letter written in longhand.

"Daisy,

I promised I would take care of you and our child, and I will. I have arranged for us to leave on Christmas Eve morn. A horse and carriage will whisk us to a better life. Please dress my son as warmly as you can for it's bound to be a cold day.

Til then,

Your very own, Ernest"

The letter trembled in my hand. "He must have killed her that same day."

"It's not enough," Robert said.

"Why? He can't recant what he wrote."

"He could say somebody else wrote it and added his name as a subterfuge. He's a trusted member of the Winchester Constabulary, Catherine. He'll need to confess."

"Well then. Let's get him to do just that. Sebastian invited him to today's festivity. Let's put our heads together and plan what to say."

But before we could do that, the sounds of an altercation reached us, likely coming from the Great Hall. We rushed out of the chapel in that direction to find Mister Seward yelling at Inspector Fallon. "You murdered my mother."

Several gentlemen, including Sebastian, Marlowe, and Hollingsworth, were trying to pull them apart.

Inspector Fallon held a sneer on his lips. "Now, lad, why would I do such a thing? I barely knew her."

"That's not true," I yelled before marching toward where they stood, right in the center of the hall, "and I have the proof. The letter you wrote to Daisy."

My hand and voice shaking, I read it out loud. Not a whisper was heard.

"You dastard," Sebastian said.

"How could you do such a horrible thing?" Margaret asked. "That poor woman."

Soon, he was surrounded by angry people, not only from the village, but our guests as well. Every last one of them yelling and screaming at him. If something wasn't done, it could easily turn into a lynch mob.

Thankfully, Robert and Mister Clapham managed to settle the crowd by promising justice would be served. If they hadn't, blood would have been surely spilled on this Christmas Day.

Retrieving a set of handcuffs from the depth of his coat, Robert fastened them around Fallon's wrists. "My name is Robert Crawford, and I'm a Chief Detective Inspector with Scotland Yard. By the authority provided to me by His Majesty, King George, I'm arresting you for the murder of Daisy Gordon."

He turned to Sebastian, "I'll need a motorcar to get us to Winchester."

Neville stepped forward. "I'll be glad to drive you, Inspector Crawford."

"Thank you," Robert said. "Mister Clapham, if you could come along."

"Glad to."

More than likely, he would provide testimony at the Winchester constabulary about everything he'd learned. Robert might be a Chief Detective Inspector, but they might not take his word for it. Regardless, he would make sure an inquest was held, and Fallon was held accountable.

"Miss Worthington, I'll need that letter."

I handed it to him.

Within a few minute, Robert, Fallon, Mister Clapham, and Neville were gone.

CHAPTER 16

A CHRISTMAS WISH

*I*N THE LATE AFTERNOON, snow started to fall. Unfortunately, that cut short the festivities as everyone wanted to return home before the village road became too treacherous to drive. Even with the drama that had ensued, all the villagers left with bright smiles on their faces. Not a surprise. Sebastian had bought enough presents for every child in the village as well as every adult. Needless to say, they were quite happy with their new duke.

As we'd had enough food and drink during the Christmas Day festivities, supper consisted of a light collation made up of cold meats, bread, pastries, coffee, and tea. No one complained, indeed we complimented the staff on their delicious Christmas Day offerings.

Since the staff deserved a well-earned rest, Sebastian gave them all leave for the next day. As it would be Boxing Day, he'd arranged gifts for them as well. He specifically told them they were neither to cook nor clean nor do any type of work.

The guests would muddle through by themselves. But many of the staff ignored the order, including Mrs. Sweetwater who served a full breakfast spread the next morning. As many of the guests were leaving, she'd determined a decent breakfast was needed before they headed to the train station.

By noon, the only ones left at Wynchcombe Castle were Sebastian and Margaret, the Worthington clan, Lady Lily, and Robert. Margaret had wished to have her family around her one last day before she assumed the Duchess of Wynchcombe duties.

Mister Clapham had departed for London along with his daughter, son-in-law, and granddaughter. Since he'd missed precious days with them while in pursuit of justice for Daisy, he would remain with them through the New Year.

Lord Marlowe and Lady Emma remained as ever unattached. She did not mention what occurred Christmas night, and, for once, I did not ask. But I caught them sharing kisses in a corner of the library. Her mother, Lady Carlyle, remained ignorant about their romance. Or, more likely, she'd chosen to ignore it and see where it led.

Lady Wakefield and Lord Newcastle promised to send us an invitation to their wedding which would be held in high summer. We would, of course, attend.

Lord Hollingsworth, Lady Melissande, as well as the entire Worthington London house staff, had also departed and were on their way back to London.

And as for Mother, she was happily making plans for the season as she'd have two young ladies to escort around town. Although Margaret had planned to take on that task, at least as far as Lady Lily was concerned, Mother had rightfully pointed out Margaret would be too busy with her new Duchess of Wynchcombe duties, finishing her studies for her Oxford degree, and planning benefits for her women's causes to shepherd Ladies Lily and Melissande through a hectic social season. So, Mother had volunteered to take on that chore. Not that it would be one for she was truly looking forward to it. With a visible sigh of relief, Margaret had accepted.

Jack Seward and John Stirling were bound for Yorkshire as Jack wished to see his old friends and enjoy time with his uncle. More than likely he would share many memories about Daisy once they had a chance to sit and talk.

"Do you think Mister Seward will return?" I asked Sebastian.

"I hope so. He's an excellent estate manager. But, of course, it will be up to him to decide. At the very least, he'll be returning for the funeral as well as the inquest."

"Did Fallon admit to the murder when you questioned him?" Margaret asked of Robert.

Following police procedure, he'd waited until they'd reached Winchester before interrogating the dastard.

"He did. He couldn't deny he'd written the letter as the handwriting matched reports he'd filed."

"But how did get that letter to Daisy?" I asked.

"By sheer accident, Daisy discovered the exit that led to the back of the castle. So, one night she borrowed one of the bicycles stored in the stable and traveled to the village. Imagine his surprise when he saw her. He thought she was gone. That's when she told him where she was staying and the way through the tunnel."

"Easy when you know it's there," I said.

"It's now sealed off," Sebastian said. "When the weather is more clement in the spring, I'll wall it off."

"Are you sure, Sebastian?" Margaret asked. "It's part of your family's history."

"I won't sleep soundly knowing someone can break into our home as easily as all that. I'll also have a stronger lock put on the kitchen door that leads to the produce garden."

Margaret did not seem to agree with his proposed course of action. But that was their problem to solve.

"So, what happened after Fallon told her about the exit?" I asked Robert.

"For the next few weeks, they had the occasional rendezvous. Those did not go well. She wished to marry to give the baby a proper name. That was the last thing he wanted as he was already courting his future wife. When he refused, she made a fatal mistake. She threatened to let everyone know he was the father. Her fate was sealed at that point. But he couldn't very well kill her while she was expecting a child. So, he waited until the babe was born. He nailed the letter you found to the tunnel door telling her to be ready. They'd agreed on communicating in that fashion. On Christmas Eve, he showed up and murdered her."

"Such a horrible thing to do," Mother said. "And then he leaves the babe alone with no one to care for him."

"He knew John Stirling and Mrs. Grimes handled Daisy's needs. So, he thought the babe would be quickly found. But it was Christmas Eve, and the staff was being run off its feet. They had no time to visit her."

"That's when the old duke heard the babe's cries and set this set of events in motion."

"If he'd given her a proper burial, we never would have found her," I said.

"He believed word would get out and everyone would think the babe was his."

"What a horrid man," Mother said. "My apologies, Sebastian. I shouldn't have said such a thing."

"No offense taken, Mrs. W, I happen to agree with you."

"He also confessed to poisoning Mrs. Sweetwater," Robert said.

"Just as I thought," I said. "But how did he break into her parlor?"

"Policemen learn all kinds of tricks. Getting into her parlor would have been child's play."

As it was late and tomorrow, we would have an early start, the party soon dispersed. Most made their way to their rooms. Robert and I, however, headed once more for the solarium.

"I'm beginning to love this room."

"Are you?"

"Yes. It's truly lovely. Cold, but lovely. In the spring, it will be a sight to behold."

"Would you like your very own solarium?"

"In your townhouse? The architecture would not allow for it."

"In a castle."

I laughed. "Planning on living in one, are you?"

A strange expression rolled over his face. "Maybe someday."

"And where would this mythical castle exist?"

"In the Cotswolds."

"Ooh, how lovely. Lord Rutledge's castle is there, isn't it? Maybe we could visit him," I said pulling him down for a kiss.

"That could be arranged." And then he kissed me, and the whole world went away.

* * *

A MURDERED YOUNG WOMAN. **Kitty's fiancé blamed for the crime. Can she catch the killer before he hangs from a noose?**

A Murder at Oxford, Book 6 in The Kitty Worthington Mysteries. Available from Amazon. https://readerlinks.com/l/2928932

England, 1924. With business booming at the Ladies of

Distinction Detective Agency and her personal life going swimmingly, Kitty Worthington couldn't be happier. But then she gets a cryptic summons from her sister urging her to come to Oxford. An urgent matter threatens someone Kitty holds dear.

Before long, Kitty learns a murder victim has been discovered, a young woman with close ties to Scotland Yard Inspector Robert Crawford, Kitty's fiancé. When alarming testimony at the inquest brands him the murderer, Kitty urges him to reveal the truth about his relationship with the murder victim. Inexplicably, he refuses to do so, leaving Kitty with no choice but to investigate.

As matters grow from bad to worse, Kitty and her team of sleuths—comprised of lords and ladies, family and friends—follow a trail of secrets and lies through the cobblestoned streets and hallowed halls of Oxford to unearth a murderer who's evaded justice far too long. For if they don't, Kitty's beloved may very well wrongfully pay with his life.

A Murder at Oxford, Book 6 in The Kitty Worthington Mysteries, a 1920s historical cozy mystery set among the rarefied atmosphere of Oxford academia, is sure to please lovers of Agatha Christie and Downton Abbey alike. https://readerlinks.com/l/2928932

* * *

Have you read the first Kitty Worthington Mystery? **Murder on the Golden Arrow**, Book 1 in the Kitty Worthington Mysteries, is available on Amazon and Kindle Unlimited readerlinks.com/l/2101140band

WHAT's a bright young woman to do when her brother becomes the main suspect in a murder? Why, solve the case of course.

England. 1923. After a year away at finishing school where she learned etiquette, deportment, and the difference between a salad fork and a fish one, Kitty Worthington is eager to return home. But minutes after she and her brother Ned board the Golden Arrow, the unthinkable happens. A woman with a mysterious connection to her brother is poisoned, and the murderer can only be someone aboard the train.

When Scotland Yard hones on Ned as the main suspect, Kitty sets out to investigate. Not an easy thing to do while juggling the demands of her debut season and a mother intent on finding a suitable, aristocratic husband for her.

With the aid of her maid, two noble beaus, and a flatulent basset hound named Sir Winston, Kitty treads a fearless path through the glamorous world of high society and London's dark underbelly to find the murderer. For if she fails, the insufferable Inspector Crawford will most surely hang a noose around her brother's neck.

A frolicking historical cozy mystery filled with dodgy suspects, a dastardly villain, and an intrepid heroine sure to win your heart. Available on Amazon and Kindle Unlimited readerlinks.com/l/2101140

ISBN-13: (EBook) 978-1-943321-18-6

ISBN-13: (Print) 978-1-943321-22-3

Hearts Afire Publishing First Edition: December 2022

CAST OF CHARACTERS

Kitty Worthington - Our amateur sleuth

The Worthington Family

Mildred Worthington - Kitty's mother
Edward Worthington - Kitty's father
Ned Worthington - Kitty's oldest brother
Richard Worthington - Kitty's next older brother, in Egypt
Margaret Worthington - Kitty's older sister, engaged to the
Duke of Wynchcombe

The Worthington Household

Betsy - Kitty's assistant at the Ladies of Distinction Detective
Agency, formerly Kitty's maid
Grace - Kitty's current maid
Mr. Carlton - the family butler
Mrs. Simpson - the family housekeeper
Neville - the family chauffeur and Betsy's beau

Mrs. Cutler - Cook and Betsy's aunt
Sir Winston - the family's beloved Basset Hound

The Wynchcombe Family

Sebastian Dalrymple - the Duke of Wynchcombe and
Margaret's fiancé
Lady Lily Dalrymple - Sebastian's sister

Wynchcombe Castle Household

Mr. Cogsworth - the castle butler
Mrs. Rawlins - the castle housekeeper
Mrs. Sweetwater - the castle cook
Mrs. Branson - newly hired cook's assistant
Mr. Seward - the Duke of Wynchcombe's estate manager

Other Notable Characters

Chief Detective Inspector Robert Crawford - Kitty's fiancé
Owen Clapham - former Scotland Yard detective inspector
who assists with investigations
Detective Inspector Fallon from the Winchester
Constabulary
Lord Marlowe - an Earl
Lord Newcastle - another Earl and Ned's friend
Lady Wakefield - widow and particular friend of Lord
Newcastle
Lavender Rose – Lady Wakefield's daughter
Lady Emma Carlyle - Kitty's friend and partner in the Ladies
of Distinction Detective Agency
Lady Carlyle - Lady Emma's mother
Lord Hollingsworth - explorer and adventurer

Lady Melissande - Lord Hollingsworth's sister

Pastor Henry Pennyworth – Pastor presiding over the wedding

Eleanor "Bumble" Pennyworth - Pastor Pennyworth's wife and Owen Clapham's daughter

Made in the USA
Las Vegas, NV
13 September 2023